I0660609

Mrs. Leith Adams

The Peyton Romance

Vol. I

Mrs. Leith Adams

The Peyton Romance
Vol. I

ISBN/EAN: 9783337052294

Printed in Europe, USA, Canada, Australia, Japan

Cover: Foto ©Andreas Hilbeck / pixelio.de

More available books at **www.hansebooks.com**

THE

PEYTON ROMANCE

BY

Mrs. LEITH ADAMS

(Mrs. R. S. DE COURCY LAFFAN)

AUTHOR OF

"BONNIE KATE," "A GARRISON ROMANCE," "LOUIS DRAYCOTT," ETC.

IN THREE VOLUMES

VOL. I.

LONDON

KEGAN PAUL, TRENCH, TRÜBNER, & CO. L^{TD}

PATERNOSTER HOUSE, CHARING CROSS ROAD

1892

This Book

IS

AFFECTIONATELY DEDICATED

TO

MY DEAR BROTHER AND SISTER,

SURGEON-COLONEL AND MRS. F. H. WELCH.

STRATFORD-ON-AVON,

June 1892.

CONTENTS.

VOLUME I.

THE PEYTON ROMANCE.

CHAPTER I.

THE OLD HALL.

THE ground sloped upwards behind the house, and here and there tall brotherhoods of firs, gathered in groups, were for ever whispering to each other, as the breeze gently stirred their dark plumed heads. Golden bracken in autumn, heaven-blue hyacinths in spring, gave colour to the underwood, while here and there a rabbit leapt, its white tail flickering among the green, and grey, and amber.

This rising background well defined the grey stone of the house, its ivy-wreathed turrets, and quaint, high-gabled roof. Below were terraced gardens, with stone balustrades, one above the other; and on the stone everywhere, that of the house and that of the terraces, the hand of Time had cunningly embroidered many devices in moss and lichen, patterns in green and yellow, and endless shades and tints of olive. Here and there the stonecrop lifted its crown of amber stars amid pale leaves, and in the niches of the balustrades wine-coloured wallflowers had taken root, waving their scented blossoms like banners year by year.

That peacocks should strut, and sun their shining necks, and spread their glorious Argus-eyed tails in such a terrace-land was naturally to be expected, and sure enough the gay bird's clarion cry, "Oh, joy! oh, joy!" was ofttimes to be heard, shriller and more piercing when the sober-coated hen marched daintily along the mossy pathways, followed by her trembling, flitting brood.

A great bloodhound, too, would often slouch and saunter up and down, or lie in the sun at the top of the wide stone steps (falling there with a deep and heavy sigh), and look scornfully at the peacocks, as who should say they really were, as a family, too vain and frivolous for anything, and not to be endured.

You could see the village of Scarsdale peeping here and there through the trees in the shallow valley, or rather depression, that lay some distance off to the right, and, at the edge of the sky, were to be seen on a clear day those billowing seas of ling, the Yorkshire Wolds.

Doubtless at one time the Hall had been spoken of as Scarsdale Hall ; but that was in the old-fashioned days, when "the county" held itself very high, and an insurmountable *chevaux de frise* of exclusiveness hedged it round. The levelling spirit that has now laid most barriers low was, however, beginning to make itself felt at the period when our story opens, and one or two glaringly white buildings had risen up on the gentle grassy slopes amid the whispering firs and swaying beeches. These "new-fangled" mansions have been built to the order of such people as a gentleman

from Australia (as the village had it) and a
large and successful manufacturer, who thought
to put a finishing gloss upon his acquired
gentility by becoming the owner of a country
seat some distance removed from the scene
of the labours that were the source of his
wealth.

These bits of local social colouring are only
put in to explain just how it was that Sir
Marmaduke Peyton's place came to be
generally spoken of as the Old Hall. There
were so many new ones about, you see.
"The Peytons?" would the wise old men
and knowing old women of the village say.
"Oh, they're some of the old gentry, you
know—the real old families, they are."
There is a fine recognition of the fitness of
things in the rural mind, and Scarsdale,
which was a sort of place betwixt and
between a village and a small country town,
rated at their exact value the glitter and
glare of the *nouveau-riches* and the dignity of
the "real old gentry," who were, perhaps, not
so profitable, but more to be proud of.   Sir

Marmaduke was the fourth baronet of the title, and tradition said that his father and grandfather had been "wild men," who dipped somewhat deeply into the family coffers, to say nothing of mortgaging the family acres. It may be that the very force of contrast—the tendency that is in every earthly influence to swing the pendulum now too far on this side, now on that—had made Sir Marmaduke what he was—a man of narrow, rigid mind, and of manners so reserved as to trench upon moroseness. He presented a strange mixture of fanaticism and worldly wisdom—a Puritanism that had become morbid, and blighted all the spontaneity and brightness of his life, tainting, alas! the lives of those about him, casting, as it were, a shadow upon them, chill and sombre; and yet a shrewdness and determination upon certain lines that startled you, as the unexpected ever must, almost making you feel as though you had received a blow in the face. A figure tall and loosely built; shaggy eyebrows set close above piercing

grey eyes, that yet at times had a far-off
look in them not wanting in pathos; fine
silken locks falling on either side a high,
narrow brow; thin lips folded close, yet in
moments of excited or troubled feeling given
to a strange convulsive flicker and working;
a voice subdued and yet sonorous—a voice
that made itself heard in a crowd of other
voices; a personality that made men say:
"Who is that?" "Can you tell me who that
is?" from which women, other than those
of his own household, shrank with a sort
of shuddering inward moan, as conscious of
some latent powers in him resembling the
fabled "evil eye." Such was Marmaduke
Peyton. If the women of his own household
shivered and moaned, they did it in the sacred
solitude of their own chambers. Pride was
bred in the Peyton blood, and seemed to
prove catching to those with whom they
intermarried. No displaying of heart-sores,
no moaning out in the open for them. But
maybe the old mullioned rooms could have
told strange stories, and the pictured dead

and gone Peytons let in to the oaken walls
looked down with pitiless smile and smirk
upon tears and moaning that told of a breaking heart.

But it will be well to get all our scenery
well set before we bring in our *dramatis
personæ*, so follow me down from one shallow
terrace to another, down the garden of the
Old Hall, and out through the massive gate,
whereon two griffins, grim and bold, hold
up a javelin apiece, and threaten all that
pass by that way. The road winds in a
gentle fall on towards the village. In early
summer the hedges on either hand are set
so thick with roses that it is like walking
between undulating lines of pink ribbon,
deftly unwinding. When you got to the
houses, some grouped and some set in rows,
you would fain hope that the inhabitants of
Scarsdale were a sober lot, for the side-walks
in the central street were elevated far above
the roadway, in some places almost as much
as a couple of yards, and surely a toper
returning home would have run great risk

of neck and limb. But the arrangement had
its advantages, since in rain or mire the said
pathways were dry and clean, and as to the
children, why, they seemed to be born subtle,
and avoided the dizzy edge as by an evolved
instinct.   This edge went by the name of the
" brink," and you might hear wary mothers
shouting to Eliza Ann or Susan Mary (double
names were all the fashion at Scarsdale) to
bring little 'Lisabeth Jane away from the
brink, or to be sure and " kitch " Sammy
by the hand, he being a toddling mite whose
nether garments were fastened with big brass
buttons right under his arms, and made him
look like a little caddis-worm set on end.
The village was near upon three miles from
the Old Hall, and only about half a mile from
the latter—maybe scarcely that—you turned
down a green and verdant lane, or rather
wide field-path, and found yourself in a place
called The Meadows. You had to pass over
a bridge to get to it, for the river made a
sudden sharp bend, and once across this you
became conscious of the whirr, whirr, whirr

of a mill, the rush of a weir, the sound of water being churned and thrashed by an ever-revolving wheel.

The Meadows was a charming place, with its rushing stream, its reedy islets and mossy creeks, beyond which a wide, shallow water-way spread out like a sheet of silver, glittering among the grassy knolls and clumps of flags and loosestrife, rippling up around the pale veronica and golden buttercups, kissing the blossoms that grew near enough to be got at. A sort of amphibious place, infinitely charming in its many varied aspects, and always musical with the low soft song of the mill, was the "Meadows." Cows, dun-coloured and white, stood half in and half out of the water, looking as if they were calmly waiting (chewing the cud meanwhile) for Cooper or Cuyp to paint them. Then there was a delightful bridge just above the mill, from which you could watch on one side the deep stillness of the mill-pool, and on the other the fume and toss of the "fall," foam-flecked and tumbling on as if in ever such a mighty hurry, showing here and there little iron grids called "slives," used to sift the jetsam and flotsam of the scud, and moss-grown piles and bars, so brightly green that they shone like emeralds in the sun. In some spots were tufts of feathery meadow-sweet, islands of sedge and rushes, where the water-rats held high festival below, while the sedge-warbler flitted like a fairy thing above. All these might be seen from the mill-bridge. Then came the mill with its *hum, hum, hum*, a great white bee that never ceased to sing.

Oh, how fair and white were its walls and floors, so that it looked like a palace of purity! How sweet and clean and wholesome it smelt as you leant your arms on the low half-door, and were conscious of the delicious dither and tremble of machinery pitilessly revolving! How like gnomes looked the miller's men, likewise powdered white going up and down the open stairways with sacks from which the white and fragrant meal dribbled slowly!

There are few spots more sweet and clean

and wholesome than a flourmill, few that so exquisitely harmonise with a fair green landscape of wood and field and stream ; while the low, ever-murmuring voice of the wheel seems to sing a soft lullaby to the ear of Nature.

One terror, however, to evil-doers was to be found at Scarsdale Mill. You stooped down to peer through a low archway in the wall, and there you saw, pent up within, prisoned in the gloom that was broken here and there by a ray of level sunlight, or the glint of broken water, a slow-revolving monster, the great black-barred wheel. This had given rise to a threat among the mothers of Scarsdale.

"Naughty childer should be scramed i' the wheel-house !"

Oh, the horror of it ! The darkness, the mystery of the dreadful fate that should befall any child of Adam thus bestowed ! No wonder little curl-crowned heads cowered under the bed-clothes, and the patchwork counterpane was pulled over frightened eyes.

Still it was a fearful joy to bend down

and gaze into that gruesome chasm ; all the more delightful if you knew you would be slapped if mother saw you.

Then the happiness of frightening other people about it was not a thing to be despised by any means. Altogether juvenile Scarsdale could ill have done without the mill—wheel and all.

From the Old Hall a narrow field-path cutting off the road wound down to The Meadows, and here might often be seen Lady Peyton walking slowly towards the cluster of cottages where the mill-hands lived, ever bound upon some sweet errand of mercy.

These cottages were as picturesque as though designed for the background of the picture, "Landscape with Cows." Vines grew, oddly enough, with great luxuriance at Scarsdale, and ran along from house to house, stretching out arms in every direction, and showing to great advantage against the white walls barred with black. Perhaps the grapes these half-wild vines bore were by no means luscious, and certainly were few and far

between, but their beautiful foliage was a
feast to the eye—a feast which had to com-
pensate for other deficiencies. One porch was
a regular Jack-in-the-green; and a little two-
roomed house, deserted and falling into cruel
ruin, had been clasped and girded about by
vine-boughs, and circled and bound with ivy,
till it looked as pretty as, or even prettier
than, its neighbours. The deserted garden
that surrounded it was a palace of delight to
the little ones, and through the rails, that were
falling apart in very inebriated fashion, their
sonsie faces would peer and peep at Lady
Peyton as she passed by with the peculiar,
dignified, sweeping gait characteristic of her
at all times.

A woman with a sorrow in her heart that
never rose to her lips. A woman with no
confidant save the God who reads all hearts
and sounds all sorrows. A woman with a
grandly outlined face, with something of the
pictured Dante in its grave and noble lines.
Yet the children did not fear her; they
stretched little hands through the bars, and

touched her gown of fine yet austere black, and she never chid them. They put forth flowers — rather drooping flowers, that had been held all too closely in little hot hands —to tempt her, and she took them with a gentle passing smile that dawned in her face like light, and then faded as a light goes out. The women curtsied as her ladyship passed, and brought their newest babies out to her to see. She would touch the little rosepink, crumpled faces with a tender hand, and ask after the mother's health or the old grandfather's ailment in a voice that told of the repression of a lifetime, yet was tuneful too, and had something of the vibration of an Æolian harp.

What was this woman's history? Had she loved with heart and soul, and then, had the fount of joy been frozen at its source, had the heart been crushed even to powder? But even in the crushing had the exquisite capability of a sympathy deep and tender been exhaled, as perfume is crushed from the spice and the flower?

Was the woman's character chastened, puri-
fied, perfected by the fire through which it
had passed ?

It must have been so.

Yet none could know or guess at the hidden
depths of life.

The woman with the black banded hair,
the dark, sorrowful eyes, and the set mouth
went on her way in, but not of, the world
around her; sustained by some hidden strength,
communing with High Heaven as never with
any of earth.

There were hints and surmises in her own
social circle, but assured knowledge there was
none. People thought her cold and self-contained, girt about with an irresistible and
queenly dignity. The gentleman from the
Antipodes, the manufacturer so happy out of
sight of his chimneys and out of hearing of his
machinery, never got what they called "any
further" with her; or, as the former jocularly
put it, it was always "as you was." He had
clapped the Lord-Lieutenant of the county
on the back—to that worthy's no small amaze-

ment; he had "chaffed" a real live Countess;
but he drew the line at the chatelaine of the
Old Hall. "Gad, sir!" he said to a kindred
spirit, "she freezes the blood in my veins."
But there was nothing chill, nothing repellent,
in Lady Peyton as she stood by the bedside
of a sick child, or clasped and held the hand
of man or woman weary and heavy laden
with the burden of a grief. Indeed, there
was nothing repellent in her at any time, for
her courtesy was polished and perfect, but yet
a barrier invincible when she chose.

No little hands were thrust through the
palings with a wilted flower, no rippling
laughter, no saucy, happy glances greeted Sir
Marmaduke as he passed on his way.

Rather the little ones ran away and peeped
from safe corners with wide eyes at the tall,
gaunt figure of the Lord of the Manor. The
flowers might lie in the great man's path,
but they were dropped from limp hands in
the hurry of flight.

Yet, for all that, Sir Marmaduke was the
"great man" of Scarsdale. There was no

one "counted so high," as the topers at the "Green Dragon" put it—no one, however wealthy or however wise.

"Him and his forbears 'has bin here so long," would the wiseacres say in between the long, hard puffs that are needed to set a pipe properly alight; "why, there beant no record o' times when there weren't a Peyton, bless yo', up at t' Ould Hall."

Thus was the Squire of the Old Hall held in estimation, yet not beloved. Thus was his wife revered, and well beloved also.

Was her self-contained, silent life the outcome of this one fact—the fact that she was the wife of Sir Marmaduke Peyton?

Was the shadow of his narrow and morose spirit ever upon her? Had he chased all the brightness from her life, crushed the song and the laughter on her lips, even in the years that were past?

Who might say?

At times the husband and wife walked together, side by side, yet strangely silent, Hound following slowly on behind. There

had been a time when two young sturdy boys
had gone on before, or, oftener still, the
younger holding his mother's hand and looking up into her face, the elder pacing staidly
by his father's side.

People called the younger "the mother's
boy," but, indeed, he was everybody's boy,
was Cyril Peyton ; he was one of those
creatures, bright as a sunbeam, who shine
alike upon the evil and the good, whom the
eye loves to follow and the heart to cherish.
As the sunbeam brightens the dark still waters
of the mountain tarn, so the love of her fair
young son touched into radiance the life of
Marion Peyton, his mother.

Her eye followed him, full of the hunger
of the heart. Every touch of her hand was
a caress. There had been a time when, a
boy of eight years, he lay at the point of
death, his lovely lips black and parched, his
eyes of golden brown unseeing, blind, and
sunken ; and some one, a villager, peering
into the empty church at eventide, was filled
with fear at sight of a figure, still as some

carved image, a figure with bowed head and
clasped hands outstretched, kneeling in the
shadow of the altar; filled still more to overflowing with dread, indeed, when a long,
quivering groan broke the stillness of the
quiet place, and the bitter cry of old, "My
son! my son!" went shuddering up to
heaven.

The boy was given back to the riven heart.
Once more he laughed to see the peacock
spread his arch of feathers, strutting on the
garden terrace; once more hung upon his
mother's hand. That mother said but little
of the almost anguish of thankfulness in her
heart. She could not endure that her joy
should be seared and blighted by words of
stern reproach from her husband's lips; by
the anathema pronounced against idol-makers,
and those who clung too closely to the things
of sense. Was not her beautiful boy a gift
from God? Why, then, might she not find
joy and gladness in such sweet possession?
That her love for him was restrained in expression, the boy soon grew to understand;

learnt, too, to restrain the expression of his
own for her, except when they were alone.
Then he would cling about her, fondle her
dear hands, kiss her pale cheeks, and pin a
posy of sweet flowers in her bosom. But
ofttimes she put these away, keeping, may be,
one wee sweet blossom to press between the
leaves of her bible.

"Flowers are not for me, my darling," she
would say, putting back the bright curls from
his brow, and looking into the sweet, laughter-
loving eyes.

When he was a very little fellow indeed he
would say—

"But God made all the pitty fowers, and
he must have made some for my movver."

But when he grew to be a tall schoolboy,
Cyril gave up such reasoning. His bonnie
face lost some of its brightness, but all the
lovingness remained.

It was gradually dawning upon him that
indeed and in truth life had "no flowers" for
that dear mother whom he worshipped with
every fibre of his young being.

Cyril had entered the shadow that brooded over the Old Hall, and was conscious of its chill.

If the boys did ill at school, if they brought home bad reports, and records of slow and unsatisfactory progress, blame was dealt out to them in fullest measure. Rightly enough too; but does not the converse hold good?

Is it well that the young heart, filled with enthusiasm, hot with ambition, resolute to achieve, should never be cheered by one hearty " Well done!"—that the eye, raised in hope to the father's face, should have to sink to the earth in disappointment, the breast to heave with the sigh that means, "Have I, then, laboured so hard in vain—does no one care?"

I remember a Scotchwoman once saying to me, "I cannot look back and remember one single instance of my father saying 'Well done!' to any one of his children;" and yet the family in question were men and women of exceptional brilliancy.

Is not this way of dealing with our children

somewhat after the fashion of those who,
being asked for bread, give but a stone to the
suppliant ? If the Father who is above
measured out such measure to us, His children,
surely we should have no sweet and sunny
days, no flowers to gladden our pleased eyes,
no birds of song to gladden our charmed ear,
no soft and silver moonlight, no radiance of
dawn—all would be grey and gloomy, just
sufficient for bare life, and for that alone.

Maybe Sir Marmaduke Peyton would better
have liked this world of ours if it had been
more after such a pattern. *Ergo* he saw no
reason to strive after making it a bright and
happy place to those to whom he had given
life. Indeed, it often seemed as though
the peacock preening itself in the sunshine,
the blaze of the wine-coloured nasturtiums,
the glory of the serried hollyhocks, the beauty
and perfume of the roses in the Old Hall
gardens, were somehow incongruous when the
owner of them all paced sombrely in their
midst. One might have imagined the peacock hurrying to hide his diminished head in

a laurel-bush, creeping in, and, ostrich-like, leaving his tail visible in sublime unconsciousness, instead of looking (as he did) as though he thought all the gardeners were maintained to keep the place in order wholly and entirely for his own pleasure and benefit. One could not have wondered if the flowers had drooped and faded, turning to bunches of rustling dry leaves in the breeze that stirred them.

Launcelot—called "Lance" for short—Sir Marmaduke's eldest son, was a moody-spirited boy, with a strong will of his own, and a passionate element in his character that was entirely absent in the younger.

The first of these attributes his father resolved to subdue—to "cast out the devil that was in possession," was the way he phrased it. But the said devil was pertinacious.

"I don't think our father is a bit like other boys' fathers; I don't think he's nice at all," said young hopeful, with a frown, and his hands well crammed into his trousers pockets.

"Perhaps he isn't," replied Cyril, reddening under the skin browned by cricket and plenty of it; "but I'm sure it would grieve mother —indeed it would, Lance, to know that we said so."

"You are always thinking of what mother would think."

"She is so dear," said Cyril, with a soft light in his eyes.

The brothers by this time were tall striplings, the elder—so folk said—the handsomer, but the younger dowered with that winning grace that is so perilous a gift.

The purity of childhood, the coming strength of manhood, sat enthroned upon his open brow, shone in his frank and lustrous eyes.

It is rare that a boy passes through boyhood's days, and touches the threshold of manhood, thus unsullied. But there are such cases for all that, and of these Cyril Peyton was one.

He was no fool, and not a bit of a "mollie." The best "forward" in his school team, a batting average of twenty-four, a mug or two enshrined in his own special room—one for the "high jump," one for the "mile;"

with such attributes and possessions he could
not well be that. He was not a brilliant
scholar, but yet above the average, and as
thorough in his work as in his games. Quite
scholar enough, in fact, for a fellow whose
father was going to buy him a commission
in Her Majesty's service as soon as he
should attain—not exactly to years of discre-
tion, but to the number of years (not very
many) at which a grateful country would
consent to be defended by him.

Sir Marmaduke had schemes for his elder
son (when that devil of which we wot should
duly be cast forth), and things were much
more likely to go smoothly with Cyril far
than with Cyril near. Lance was not im-
pressionable, and had no great depths of
tenderness in his nature; but, somehow, he
was ofttimes influenced by his brother, even
when he laughed or even jeered at him, which
was not seldom.

"You're the 'good boy' of the family," he
would say with a nasty sneer; but yet he
always realised the fact that Cyril was the

"bright boy" of the family too; the light
and joy (there was not much else of that
kind) of Lady Peyton's life.

Lance was not jealous of this.

He thought his mother was, by nature, given
to the sentimental, and had only been drilled
into common sense because his father kept the
upper hand, and never allowed any nonsense.

This was his cheerful way of putting it.

That "the boy" (Cyril was always "the
boy," as if there were no other boy) was
also inclined to sentiment was undeniable.
Lance had shrewd suspicions that when they
were alone together they were very sentimental indeed—this mother who had been
repressed into common-sense, and the boy
whom nobody could repress.   Indeed, the
task would have been very much like trying
to stem a bright and sparkling stream by
catching it in your fingers.

Yes, Cyril would be much better away,
there could be no doubt about that, thought
Sir Marmaduke.   A regiment on foreign service would be the best *oubliette* possible.

Letters were harmless things compared with the electric power of personal influence; nor was the charm of Cyril's look, and voice, and manner a thing that could be written down in black and white. It was a thing intangible, irresistible, spiritual.

CHAPTER II.

In order to introduce one of the personages of our story in a befitting manner, I have to put the clock back a little.

We find ourselves in the fitful shine of a morning following upon a night of storm, and wind, and rain.

The leaves of the heavy shrubs round about the study window at the Old Hall glistened with the April brightness of smiles and tears. Here and there tall flowers lay prostrate, beaten down, bemired, broken; while the head-gardener wandered about disconsolate, like the celebrated Peri, not because he could not get in at the gate, but because his paradise was so cruelly despoiled.

Even yet the gale had hardly sobbed itself quiet, but every now and again suffered quite

a relapse, sighing hard among the many
gables, and dashing the rain-wet leaves
against the windows.

Sir Marmaduke and Lady Peyton had
dined out the night before—a night, as the
coachman observed, "not fit to turn a dog
out in"—had attended one of those solemn,
exclusive county dinners that have something
funereal in their state, and recall to the observant mind the saying that the English,
as a nation, take their pleasures sadly.

No freaks, quips, or cranks of the lively
Australian, no inflated pomposity of the
aspiring manufacturer, had broken the staid
monotony of the entertainment in question.
The painted ancestors and ancestresses on
the walls of the banqueting chamber were
scarcely less sombre than the guests upon
whom they looked with calm, observant eyes.
One glorious exception, the picture of a
certain lovely countess, with alluring smile
and dress, looked quite improper by her contrast to the frigid ladies around her and
below. To Sir Marmaduke the occasion had

appeared one of unwonted and unadvisable
dissipation, a departure from the usual routine
that had been undertaken from motives of
policy, and was not to be lightly repeated.

He sat alone in his study next morning—
a dark-panelled room, with burnished silver
sconces branching out on either side the high
carved mantel—chewing the cud of uncheer-
ful reflections. It was recognised in the
household that the "master" was in a more
than usually trying frame of mind. At no
time was any member of it ardent to enter
that stronghold, the panelled room. At all
times were they ardent to depart from it,
being once in; indeed, on one occasion a
stableman had up for correction was seen
holding parley with the foe, with all his body
"slithered," as the housekeeper put it, out
into the passage, and only a hand and arm
(the former spasmodically clutching the
handle) visible to the stern eye of Sir
Marmaduke.

On this particular day, however — not a
very auspicious time, one would have thought

—a certain young groom, called Jem Dorrington, saw fit to approach the dreaded portal, rap softly on the panel, and enter at the sharp " Come in" that followed.

" Well, what is it?" said Sir Marmaduke, with the air as of one who should say, " I trust there is an adequate and sufficient motive underlying this intrusion"—an air that takes the wind out of any one's sails about as effectually as possible.

But Dorrington held his ground.

" Please, Sir Marmydook," he said, advancing well into the gleam of the fitful sunshine, "this has taken the liberty to be born."

" This" was apparently a soft ball of red-brown plush that lay in the hollow of the man's arm. When you looked closer into it you saw that it had two absurdly exaggerated pendant ears and a pair of closed eyes, only discernible by a bright tawny spot above each.

In the best made case-armour some spot is vulnerable.

Sir Marmaduke Peyton had a soft place in his heart for—dogs.

"Dear me!" he said, peering from under his bushy brows at the bunch of brown plush; "it is a bloodhound puppy."

"Yes, Sir Marmydook; and the bitch is dead."

"Where did she come from?"

"We can't none of us tell that, Sir Marmydook. Jennings thought as how he heard some soft-footed beast a-following of the carriage last night, but he never ketched a sight on it, which seemed strange like. He'd a fancy, too, as he heard a kind o' keenin' as he went round home, but you know what last night was, Sir Marmydook, and it wur hard to tell what was wind and what was dogs."

"Quite so!"

That the master should be thus good and gracious appeared to Dorrington as little short of a miracle.

He took up an easier attitude, cuddling the soft brown thing that called itself a bloodhound puppy up to the bosom of his striped waistcoat.

"Well, Sir Marmydook, there she lay—a creetur nought but skin and boans, as must have wandered days and nights, an' miles an' miles, and lost her own self, and gone wi' an empty"—here Dorrington hesitated a moment, as if the next word was perhaps hardly just the thing for the present company—"an empty belly, beggin' your pardon, Sir Marmydook, or not far off it—there she lay, right forenenst the fowlhouse, sheltered like, and this bit of a hobjeck alongside of her. It was I as come upon her fust, and, if you'll believe me, she gev' me a look same as a Christian might ha' done, kinder tellin' me for to tak' care on t' little 'un, and then she licked it, soft like, just onc't, and 'er 'ed fell like a lump o' lead, and she wur dead, Sir Marmydook."

Sir Marmaduke cleared his throat, then the softened mood of a moment was gone.

"Let the little animal be taken care of," he said, taking up his paper to indicate that the interview was over. "See that it is taken care of."

And that was how Hound came to the Old
Hall. Not a very dignified entry, perhaps,
and having about it a distinct spice of the
foundling; but through that humble beginning into what a paradise for dogs did he
enter!

True, at first the peacock was a burden
to him, and a jackdaw, beloved of Dorrington,
put many indignities upon him in the stable-
yard, insults that were hard to bear, such as
pecking his hind-legs in unwary moments,
or perching on his head when he was wrapped
in gentle slumber.

Still, these were but specks upon the sun
of his content, for the bloodhound-puppy con-
trived to edge himself in everywhere, even
into the sacred precincts of the master's
study, where he would lie curled up upon
the wolf-skin rug, or squatted under the
black oak writing-table, and no man said
aught unto him. His legs were, for a time,
apparently hardly under his own control, and
his feet several sizes too big for him; in fact,
Hound was a hobbledehoy, and at what is

called the awkward stage of life; but this passed, as pass it will both with the human and canine animal, and as the tawny creature took his walks abroad, or posed as a lion couchant on the top of the terrace steps, there could be seen no nobler specimen of his breed.

The peacock no longer made long necks at him, investigating him as a sort of natural curiosity, or put up his tail-feathers, stamping and rustling as who should say, "What do you think of that, sir?" but rather gave him a wide berth; and as to the jackdaw, why, that aggravating beast never gave him a chance now, but kept well out of harm's way, opening his beak wide, and making horrible noises in his throat, but always taking these insulting measures when perched above the stable-door, or in some other un-get-at-able place.

Hound was a happy, placid creature, it must be confessed, and as true an aristocrat among dogs as the master of the Old Hall among men. His temper was hard to rouse, and he was the gentlest of playfellows to

children, but there were deep passions locked
in his mighty chest, and if occasion rose
worthy of so much expenditure of nervous
force, he could roar you, not exactly as a
sucking-dove, but with a prolonged ringing
bay, that called up to your mind gruesome
stories you had read of the chase in the
Dismal Swamp, when the hunted thing was
a man, and the cry of the pursuing hound as
the crack of doom to his tortured ears.

When Hound was just emerging from the
age of puppydom a mighty event took place
in his life. He noticed a sort of subdued
bustle in the household, and grew restless,
as dogs will under such circumstances. If he
had been a terrier, he would have run hither
and thither like a ferret, poking his nose into
everything; but *noblesse oblige*, and being
what he was, he simply lounged in a stately
manner from one place to another, inspecting
Mrs. Dutton, the housekeeper, and, as it were,
questioning her with his great golden-brown
eyes, until that worthy woman forgot her
gentility and cried—

"Drat the dog! What's he after? He'll
speak one of these days, you'll see, like Mr.
Balaam's ass, and I hope you'll all remember
I said so, that's all."

It struck Hound that the only person who
seemed to have nothing to do with the fuss
was Sir Marmaduke himself, so he trotted in
to look that potentate over, hoping, no doubt,
to reduce him to the same abject condition
as Mrs. Dutton. But Sir Marmaduke was
inscrutable. His head was leaning on his
hand, his shaggy brows showed a deep line
between them. He had no notice to spare
for dogs or men, so Hound curled up his nose
to show his contempt for things in general,
and trotted out again. Coming upon Lady
Peyton sitting on one of the terrace-seats, he
saw that there were tears shining in her gentle
eyes, and, with the quick sympathy of his
kind, laid his great head in her lap, and licked
her hand. But though she was tearful, she
was smiling too, like an April day, so Hound
wagged his tail, to be in tune with both
moods. Lady Peyton was watching eagerly

down the long and winding carriage-way, and
the hand against which the dog had laid his
head trembled with suppressed eagerness.

" I wonder what Cyril will think of you ? "
she said, looking down at the wistful face
that did everything but speak, and though
Hound could not, of course, tell what her
words meant, he pricked his ears up square,
and was all on the alert.

And this was what happened.

The high dogcart, with its grand grey
mare, came tooling past the lodge, and a tall,
supple figure, hardly waiting for the speed to
slacken, sprang to the ground, quite unheed-
ing the old coachman's remonstrance, rushed
along the terrace, caught Lady Peyton in a
pair of strong young arms, and then cried out
in a clear, ringing voice—

" Hallo, mother ! What's this you've got
here ? "

" This " was Hound ; the second time in
his young puppy-life that he had been desig-
nated by the demonstrative pronoun in question. " This " was highly delighted at being

taken so much notice of, and pranced in a sort of dignified and elephantine manner round his new friend.

A second figure advanced in more leisurely yet still cordial manner to greet Lady Peyton, and Hound was introduced to the notice of the young heir of the Old Hall and all the land pertaining thereunto. But the dog had neither eyes nor ears save for the first-comer. He never had eyes or ears, to speak of, for any one else any more.

He was a one-ideaed dog, and the one idea was dominant, ruling all the rest.

Said Mrs. Dutton—

"Since our young gentlemen came home from taking the tower"—Dutton spoke as though Lance and Cyril had been engaged in the siege of some redoubtable fortress, instead of spending a year in foreign parts under the scholarly guidance of a tutor—"that there dog has never been an inch away from Master Cyril as he could help."

As for Dorrington, he scratched his head, perhaps to enliven the somewhat dormant brain within, and, cap in hand, made bold to ask for an opinion upon his find.

" What do you think of t' pooppy, Maister Cyril?" he said.

"Well," said Cyril laughing, "he's hardly a puppy now, Dorrington; he's a fine specimen of his kind, and no mistake, and does you credit."

"The mother wur a gran' dawg," said Dorrington; "'twere a sin to see her lyin' dead, so lean and 'lorn, that it wur."

"The puppy fell into good hands any way, and seems to have taken a kind of fancy to me."

Jem Dorrington made no reply to this. That any created thing should look on Master Cyril and not take a fancy to him was beyond the power of the simple soul to imagine.

"Why, in coorse, the dawg took a loikin' to 'im," he said subsequently to a fellow-groom; " who wouldna?"

But at the time he only turned his cap in his hands, looked scrutinisingly at the lining, and ventured what seemed to him a bold and brazen request.

"Maister Cyril," he said, more than ever interested in the cap-lining—indeed, turning it completely inside out, "I'd take it mighty kind if you'd speak a word or two to Mr. Jennings for me."

"Have you been in trouble, Dorrington?"

"No, sir; it's not that. Since that bit of a trouble you got me out of, two year back and more, I've kept myself pretty square. If you could take the trouble to speak up for a poor chap like me, 'twas the least the poor chap could do to keep hisself clear for the future, and I've done it, sir—I have, indeed. Mr. Jennings can tell you my 'osses shines like lookin'-glass; you might see yerself in 'em any day, an' if I take my pint at the Golden Crown, I take no more. Your kindness made a changed man of me, Maister Cyril."

"Well, then, what is it you want me to do now?"

"Well, sir, it's this: if I was breeksed and

topped I could follow on to you, either on the road or in the field, and be no shame to you. It seems a deal to arst, Maister Cyril, but it 'ud be a crown o' rejoicin' to me, as you may say, and I'd serve you faithful, no fear but I would."

It will be anticipated that Jem was "breeksed" and "topped," and thus gorgeously caparisoned, appeared riding Mr. Cyril Peyton's "spare horse" during the next season's hunting, to his own unspeakable delight, and the envy of his fellows. Indeed, he gradually emerged from comparative obscurity into being looked upon as "Mr. Cyril's own man," and in his own way the world held no more contented being.

Meanwhile Hound had also presumed upon endless privileges as the guerdon of his devotion to Sir Marmaduke's younger son, and his mighty form might be seen nightly couched on the mat outside Cyril's door.

At this Mrs. Dutton, rustling in black silk and stately in a blonde lace cap with infinite streamers, had shaken her head.

It was against rules for dogs to sleep in the house.

"Now, Dutty, my own sweet Dutty, you can't find in your heart to be angry with anything I do," said Master Cyril; and Dutton bridled, and said—

"La me! what a way the boy has with him, to be sure!"

And Hound did exactly what he liked, which consisted in never being a yard away from his chosen master's side if he could help it. He patronised the rest of the household; was gentle and caressing to my lady, condescendingly polite to Sir Marmaduke and Lance, and evidently had a high opinion of Dorrington; but "the god of his idolatry" was that sweet-voiced, golden-haired, bright-eyed boy, at whose side he took such endless rambles in the Meadows, round by the mill, and down, down, down where the river widened and became a restless, roaring torrent, and the fish leapt flashing and glistening in the sunlight. This was miles below Scarsdale, and in summer-time, when the

waters were not so deep and turbulent, a very
paradise for fishermen, the pleasant rattle of
whose reels would mingle with the chirp of
the sedge-warbler and the gurgling song of
the blackcap.

"Foreign lands are all very well," said
Cyril one night, "and Lance and I had a fine
time of it, taking the 'tower,' as Dutton calls
it, to say nothing of learning to 'parley-voo'
like a couple of natives. But 'there's no place
like home' all the world over; is there, old
boy ? Why, such a ramble as you and I have
had to-day is worth all——"

Cyril speaking thus to Hound, stopped short
all at once.

Sir Marmaduke had raised his head from
his book, and was looking fixedly at his
younger son. Lady Peyton, too, found her
eyes drawn to her husband's face, and drew
a long breath.

Cyril was so heedless, so imprudent! He
knew how much his father hated what he
called "aimless chatter," and yet that dear
tongue of his would run on, on, on, just as if

he and she—they two—were alone! Would he never be warned?

Then the clear, hard, metallic voice of her husband fell upon her ear, and she clutched the table tight to keep down the passion and the pain within her.

"I trust your dislike to foreign lands, Cyril, is but a thoughtless prejudice, and one that will pass away, because I have been corresponding with the military authorities respecting the purchase of your commission——"

"Father!"

"Do not interrupt me. You did not suppose I was going to keep you here idle all your life? That would be to put you in the power of the great tempter, and to risk your eternal welfare. With your brother it is different; his work in life is to learn to come after me. Already he has mastered many details of the management of the estate; his time will never hang heavy on his hands."

"Father, I never expected or wished to live idle here or anywhere else. I have always expected to be a soldier—loved to think I

should be one; but this is so sudden. My
mother——"

"Your mother is fully aware that a woman
cannot keep her sons tied to her apron-strings
when they grow to man's estate."

The manner in which this was said accen-
tuated its offensive tone, and the red blood
rose to the margin of Cyril's crisp curls.

As for Lady Peyton, she might have been
a statue, so still was she, so immovable. She
did not even raise her eyes to the troubled
face of the boy she adored.

Why, indeed, should she?

Did she not see it in her mind's eye? Did
she not know it off by heart?

How often had she seen it looking up into
her own for counsel and comfort in the days
that were past?

The quiet, icy tones of the head of the
household flowed on.

"I am using my influence, which you
know is not small, to get you placed in a
good regiment."

Then they knew that the whole thing was

as good as done. A tremor passed over the
mother, and Lance, who had been sitting in
the far window, started to his feet.

"It is the 97th Regiment of Foot, com-
manded by my old friend Colonel Venables,
who is at present home on leave — a fine
corps, with about five years still to serve in
India, and then some prospect of a Mediter-
ranean station."

At this, absolute silence; Lady Peyton
with down-dropped eyes and a face that
showed like a waxen mask in the gathering
dusk; Lance watching his mother intently;
Cyril pale, but with the light of resolve and
courage shining in his eyes, and the hand
that rested on the table clenched.

It had all come so suddenly—so like the
lightning's flash. He knew there was no
appeal; indeed, the love of adventure that
sleeps in every manly heart was stirring in
his breast; but——

There was one thing he dared not look
upon—his mother's face.

"If you will come to my study," said Sir

Marmaduke, "I will show you the papers and give you further particulars, and we can talk things over."

He left the room, followed by Cyril, who never once turned to look upon the still form of the woman who bore him.

At the study-door Sir Peyton motioned to his son to enter, and then closed the door, shutting out Hound, who, true to his determination never to be away from his master's side if he could help it, had followed the pair.

It was significant of much, this shutting out of the faithful dog.

Home, its ties and its simple pleasures, were to be things of the past to Cyril Peyton.

Meanwhile, in the morning-room, with its deep mullioned windows, that gave such sweet glints of mead and field and dark-leaved sweeping cedar, the mother and the elder son stood face to face; for Lady Peyton had risen to her feet and moved towards the casement, making a quick gesture with her hand which Lance as quickly understood. He set the window back upon its staple, and

let the crisp evening air fan her pale cheek
and the wan brow, whereon the sweat had
beaded near the bands of her braided hair.
As he passed his arm about her shoulders
he felt her tremble, and her eyes looked into
his with the pathetic pleading you may see
in those of a wounded animal. As he placed
her gently in one of the low cushioned seats
that were made in the niches of the window,
Hound, giving a deep, gurgling sigh, laid his
great head on her knee.

How wonderful is the sympathy of the
dog for man! How keen is the instinct
with which he recognises the mood of joy
or sorrow, reflecting it in his big loving heart
as in a mirror!

Lady Peyton laid her hand on the wrinkled
tawny forehead.

"You and I shall miss him, Hound, shall
we not? We shall listen for the sound of
his footstep, and we shall not hear it."

"Mother," cried Lance, shaken for once
out of his moody reserve, "do not look so
broken-heartedly. I have not been all to

you that I might—I know it; but I will try, I will indeed. It is hard on you, all this—and to come so suddenly, without warning, without hint or preparation. Still, of course, we knew the boy must go some time."

The tears were coursing down her cheeks, a rare emotion indeed with her; and Hound, feeling that something very desperate was going on, lifted his muzzle and gave a long whining cry.

The wind that swayed the plumed heads of the larches outside echoed it back again, keening round the gables, and the long arms of the ivy and the woodbine beat against the panes like hands in desperation.

It was closing in for a wild storm-tossed night, but not more wild, not more storm-tossed than was the heart of the woman who gazed out into it through the mist of her own tears.

"Did you see that he—Cyril—dare not look at you? Mother, do you know why? He knew that if you broke down, if you showed any feeling, it would bring upon you——"

But she made a sudden gesture as though she were pushing something away from her, and he was silent; the rest of the sentence choked in his throat.

For years this weary woman had fought the battle that Fate had thrust upon her; she had struggled to prevent blame of the father passing the lips of the children; she had striven to live up to her own stern ideal of duty. She was not going to turn coward even now in the hour of her bitter trial.

Her gesture was supreme, commanding.

Lance dared not defy her in that mood. He turned to the window, drumming on the pane to relieve his impatience under a restraint he could not resist.

There is a stillness that is yet a cry; a silence that holds a deeper sadness than many words.

Such a stillness, such a silence, came into the life of Lady Peyton.

LIBRARY
UNIVERSITY OF ILLINOIS

Into the day on which her son Cyril left
his home for a foreign land were crowded
the bitterness and experiences of a lifetime.
Some live and die and do not suffer as she
suffered then. It was early morning when
the boy went away, and some pitying spirit
seemed to paralyse her memory, so that she
could not recall the last awful moments—the
clutch of his hand that grew to hers, the
death-cold touch of his lips, the long-drawn
sobs that rent his young heart as he kissed
and clasped her, calling her by every sweet
and tender name.

Then some one—surely Lance—drew him
away, and she found herself on her knees
with her face crushed against the window.
This was at early dawn of the day that was
a lifetime measured by its pain. Not one
word of help or sympathy came from the
one from whom she had the best right to
look for both. Lance had gone with his
brother to Southampton, there to see him
embark.

There was no one—no one—to solace her.

save poor Hound, who stood in sore need of comfort himself.

And the light of her life had gone out. That she was brave—wonderfully, heroically brave—goes without the saying.

But as the day waned her strength seemed to go from her. At all times of trouble the approach of night is dreaded, for when the world around us is silent our hearts speak more audibly, and we cannot choose but hear.

Lady Peyton, wrapped closely in her hooded cloak (it was early autumn, and the air was thick with falling leaves), paced the terrace. A weird grey figure in the gathering gloom, she might have been the wraith of some dead and gone Peyton visiting the scenes of her earthly life. Assuredly no visitant from the shadowy land could have shown more palely, looked forth with more weary, sorrow-laden eyes.

Suddenly, as she turned, her husband faced her.

"Marion," he said, speaking with stern, reproving voice, "you are showing a rebellious and unchastened spirit. Rather should you rejoice in humble thankfulness that you are checked in a long career of idolatry. Your prayer should be——"

She turned upon him like a tigress robbed of her young. She knew that in the sackcloth and ashes of self-reproach and the bitterness of regret should she pay the price of the momentary yielding to the passion within her, and yet for once nature and her own heart prevailed.

"My prayer is that I may live to see my boy again. My whole life will be a prayer until we meet once more—my boy and I."

"Your boy!" he hissed between his teeth. "Say rather your idol—the sin of your life, the creature whom you have exalted above the Creator, the thing you have set between yourself and your God."

She turned upon him a face marble in its pallor and rigidity.

"He be my judge; to Him will I stand or fall, not to you—not to you; and all my life, every day of it, every hour of it,

I will pray to Him to give me back my
boy."

Her voice, thrilled through with an unspeakable pain and longing, seemed to creep
like some eerie, uncanny thing out among the
shadows.

Even he, whose heart was as the nether
millstone, felt and recognised that she was
beyond the power of further words to torture.
She had reached that stage of suffering in
which the sufferer may say, "Do with me as
you will; you cannot make things worse with
me than they are."

He turned and left her, a grey figure in the
grey of the gloaming; a captive that, for once,
had escaped his grasp, a bird that had flown
beyond where his hand could reach it.

On his way to the house he met Mrs.
Dutton, who, dropping him a reverence,
stepped aside to let him pass.

Her eyes were swollen and red with
weeping.

"I was seeking my lady," she said; "I fear
things are going very badly with her."

And then her voice broke, and she put up her white frilled apron to her eyes.

"Lady Peyton is on the terrace," he said as he passed on.

There was bitterness—nay, the very gall of bitterness in his breast.

What was this boy —shallow, frivolous, dowered only with the favour that is deceitful and the beauty that is vain,—that all hearts should cling to him, all eyes become blind with tears because he had passed from their sight?

Sir Marmaduke sought the retreat of his own special room, and, once there, opened drawer after drawer, scattering papers right and left upon the long oak table.

In these he strove to find forgetfulness, poring over them, comparing them, making notes here and there; but the image of the boy with the bright curls and the winsome smile came between him and them. He was vexed with the gentle wraith of the son he had slighted from boyhood—the boy whom he held in contempt, yet was, unconsciously to himself, bitterly jealous of.

Even hatred arose in his heart as he thought of the silent meal of that evening, the dead-white face of his wife opposite him, and an angry recognition in himself that even the servants who waited round the table were on her side—were, in their own humble way, anxious to show their sympathy with and for her.

It was as if everything round about him cried "Cyril! Cyril!" nothing but "Cyril!"

All at once a long keening cry, a cry such as some banshee might utter to foretell death or misfortune, rang through the house.

Sir Marmaduke raised his head and listened intently.

His fancy—he owned to being pitifully un-nerved to-night — might have played him false. He had heard of such things.

But no!

Again and yet again rang out that plaint of woe.

It came from right overhead.

Cyril's room was overhead.

In a moment he had opened the door,

passed on quickly up the wide oak stairway that was black with age, and had reached the door of the room that had been his son's.

There on the threshold lay, or rather crouched, the mighty bloodhound, his muzzle raised, his eyes wild, staring, and tearful, as it is given to the eyes of such dogs to be, filled with a frenzy of love and loss and longing.

Just as Sir Marmaduke reached the door, once more the great tawny head was lifted high, and the wild keening echoed down the vaulted corridor.

The butler and one or two other servants had hastened up at the sound of the dog's cry and the master's hurried step, and to them Sir Marmaduke spoke.

"Fetch a rope, some of you," he said. "The dog has no business here."

Some excuses were faltered forth. It seemed that Mr. Cyril had liked to have Hound near him at night, and Mrs. Dutton had said she "didn't mind."

Sir Marmaduke might have been deaf for

any notice he took of what they said; and
Sir Marmaduke might have been dead or
miles away for any notice the dog took of
him.

They slipped the rope under Hound's collar
—the collar that Cyril had been so proud of—
and then looked at the master to see what
was to be done next.

" Take him to the stable-yard."

The dog looked with wonder and dignity
from one to the other of those who dragged
him on, and strained back against the rope.

The men, too, looked at each other.

" What was going to be done with Master
Cyril's dog ? "

Sir Marmaduke made for the big hall, took
down a heavy hunting-whip, and came out
upon the stones of the yard, where overhead
the glimmer of a swinging-lamp lit up the
strange scene.

" Tie him up to that staple," he said, pointing to an iron in the wall.

Then the lash fell heavily on the dog's
quivering flesh, blow upon blow and stroke

upon stroke. I read once the story of an old worn-out mastiff who was stoned to death by some cruel Italians. The story said that the creature faced his assailants all the time, never once giving tongue, but meeting his fate with a calm courage that might well have touched even their hard hearts. It was like that with Hound.

He shivered as the thong curled about his limbs, and looked with dumb questioning at his tormentor; but of sound made he none, save one long sobbing sigh as Sir Marmaduke flung the whip away from him.

"Tell Dorrington to take special charge of the dog," he said, "and see that he does not get into the house again at night."

There were looks interchanged, and a helper, looking horribly frightened, was shoved to the front.

"Please, Sir Marmydook," he said, shuffling uneasily from one foot to the other, and pulling off his cap, and even pocketing it in his strivings after politeness, "Dorrington's gone."

"Gone!"

The word rang out like a clarion, and went through the unfortunate stableman like a pistol-shot, but he stood to his colours.

"Yes, Sir Marmydook; he's 'listed, has Dorrington. You see, he'd got used to follerin' on to Maister Cyril, and somehow he couldn't get out of the way of it; so he's gone to be a soldier in foreign parts—same as Maister Cyril, Sir Marmydook."

CHAPTER III.

BETWEEN the Old Hall and the village stood Scarsdale Rectory ; not an even "between" by any means, since the Rectory touched, as it were, the skirts of the village, a straggling house or two saving it from isolation.

The church itself, nobly elevated, with high stone walls forming a square plateau on which it sat enthroned, churchyard and all, owned a peal of bells whose sweet and mellow voices made ever-welcome music in the ears of the passers-by.

For miles round, the tall and stately spire that held these messengers of music could be seen against the sky, peering above the wooded meads and fields, and rising heaven-wards as who should fain remind the beholder of the sanctity of earth's fair beauty, and the homage due to the Maker and the Giver of all good.

You entered the churchyard by a flight of steep stone steps, that were somewhat of a trial to the more aged of the congregation. Wandering among the flower-decked graves, you could look down on what was called Lower Scarsdale, and across a wide shallow depression, filled with streets and all the shops the place boasted, to Higher Scarsdale, where might be seen the field in which the young athletes of the neighbourhood were wont to display their cricketing prowess before admiring rustic eyes.

At the foot of the church steps stood the schools, neat buildings that on Sundays resounded with the sound of many little voices singing simple and familiar hymns, and where, on a sunny afternoon, the curate was apt to be waylaid by aspiring clergy-ladies, and wiled, if possible, into a stroll in the fields beyond the village.

No one would have ventured to waylay the Rector; indeed, on more than one occa-

sion his portly presence had been known to
put certain daring adventuresses to flight, and
cut short intended rambles, and possible sub-
sequent lingerings over tea and muffins.

His curt "Good-afternoon, Mr. Westerton,"
was enough to send the curate flying to his
lodgings like a startled rook to its elm, and
make the female bosom conscious of a sensation as though a pane of glass were set
therein ; thoughts, designs, and aspirations
showing as plainly as the goods in a shop-
window.

Not that the Rev. Reginald Wentworth
Darling was either a despot or a marplot, but
his kindly soul looked out of observant eyes,
and before the calm sagacity of their glance
disguises were given to shrivel up and wither
away, and designers to become as balloons
out of which the gas has ignominiously
escaped, leaving flabbiness and collapse behind.   Mr. Darling wore his grey-flecked hair
rather long, and his well-rounded cheek and
finely-cut chin clean shaven.   He was a man
with a keen sense of humour, and not guilt-

less of an occasional repartee, at which times
his face would light up with all the light-
hearted glee of a schoolboy. He was proud
of his church, and the world held for him no
sweeter music than the sound of its mellow
chimes. When the ringers managed to achieve
a rendering—rather lame and halting, it must
be confessed—of "Home, Sweet Home" and
"Abide with Me," he would stand in an
ecstasy, beating time—rather intermittent
time—with his folded *pince-nez*. He would
escort strangers over the church, uncover
one or two fine brasses as if the earth contained no greater treasures, expound to them
the ancient squint in the chancel, and display the glimpses of a hidden Norman arch
belonging to an older edifice upon the ruins
of which the present one had arisen. Then
he would take them into the churchyard,
and point with outstretched hand to the
panorama surrounding them on every side
—the clustering houses, gathered, as it were,
at the feet of the church, like children about
the mother's knee; the fields beyond; the

clustering woods in the distance; the glint of the silver river winding through the meadows; and, nearer at hand, the red gables of his own home showing bravely among the larches.

When people asked him what was the elaborate, glaringly white building on a certain eminence, he told them briskly and gladly about the Queensland squatter, his generous charities, his hearty ways; and when they asked about the great manufacturer's abode, he had something good to say of him too—how he encouraged the choir, and gave them a treat in summer-time at that big mansion of his, and how they looked forward to it all the rest of the year.

But if anything was said about the Old Hall, the Rector had but little to say.

"It is a fine old place, the family seat of the Peytons. It shows picturesquely from here, does it not? nestling among those pines and grand old copper-beeches, and backed by the rising hill."

That was all. Never a mention of any

member of the family of the Peytons—never
a word as to their qualities, good or bad.

He would as soon have thought of commenting upon the peculiar traits of his own
wife and daughter, would the Rev. Reginald
Wentworth Darling, as of discussing those of
Lady Peyton or her belongings.

The Hall was sacred ground to him. Had
he not there year by year, watched that
terrible tragedy, the breaking of a woman's
heart, and, alas ! been able to do little else
but watch ?

What should make any one more sacred
to us than the knowledge of their sorrows ?
What should bind them more closely to our
hearts ?

It was little indeed by word of mouth that
the good Rector of Scarsdale had gained his
insight into the life and trials of Sir Marmaduke Peyton's wife. It was rather by the
powers of intuition that were his, by reason
of the constant, loving study of humanity,
for the sake of, and in the spirit of, the
Master he served, that permeated his whole

life. To follow in that Master's footsteps, to bind up the broken-hearted, to put a hand to every burden, small or great, that bowed the shoulders and oppressed the heart—these were the aims of a life pure and beautiful in itself, and giving out light and strength and healing to others.

To the true minister (a word which perhaps means more than has ever yet been defined) there is no sharper sorrow than the realisation that, near him, yet beyond his touch, lies a grief he cannot heal; that close at hand, yet hemmed around by barriers that cannot be set aside, a battle is being waged in which he cannot strengthen the weak hands or confirm the feeble knees.

Besides, to a chivalrous man, a woman's reserve is a sacred thing; and it may be said that never, even in his own thoughts, had Mr. Darling allowed himself to pry into the domestic relations or affairs of his parishioners. He was at all times ready to be found, if sought out as a friend and counsellor, but never fell into the weakness of offering advice unasked. He realised also that a woman who takes any one into her confidence against her husband comes down a step or two from the high pedestal of her perfect womanhood. That Marion, Lady Peyton, was one to draw the mantle closely over her own troubles—one to suffer, nay, to die, in silence, if needs be, he also quickly realised.

There was one help he could give her—one he did give her, and in no stinted measure. He could pray for her as one of those whom, being distressed indeed, he would fain commend to the Fatherly goodness of the Creator and Preserver of all men, entreating Him to comfort her according to her necessities.

With Sir Marmaduke himself the Rector's relations were strained, and such as often called for much diligent forbearance. Yet a great and abounding pity mingled with his condemnation of much that was said and done at the Old Hall. Astute as well as gentle and pitiful, Wentworth Darling recognised the fact that the morose and silent Lord of the Manor had drifted into such

narrow subjection to bigotry and prejudice,
had so dressed up this narrowness and this
prejudice in the form of a self-made and
comfortless religion, that his whole life and
mind had become stunted and deformed;
that, finding neither peace nor beauty in
the world around him, he resented the sight
of others smiling in the sunshine, and was
thus quick to adopt a distorted creed, whose
chief dogmas taught that to rejoice was sin,
and to be content sensuality.

Many times and oft did the Rector deeply
sorrow over this state of matters. He felt
like a man who, holding a cup of clear and
sparkling water in his hand, sees another
parched with thirst, and yet cannot prevail
upon him to put his dry and burning lips
to the overflowing brim; or like one who,
carrying a sure staff wherewith to climb the
steep declivities and stony defiles of a toil-
some journey, cannot induce a fellow-traveller,
footsore, wounded, infinitely weary, to lean
upon it for a while, and so find renewed
strength and comfort.

As to the boys, Lance and Cyril (they always seemed boys to him, since he had watched them grow from babyhood, and always had a difficulty in realising their adolescence), it would be rash to assert that no favouritism lurked in the good Rector's bosom.

He was but a man after all, and had his weaknesses, as all have.

> " Men are not angels, as we know,
> Because they do not make them so,"

And really such little weaknesses as those of the reverend gentleman in question were such loveable things, one would hardly like him to have been without them.

Was it not natural that a boy whom no one could look upon without feeling a smile of pleasure creeping round their lips and lighting up their eyes, should creep close, close, into the very recesses of the Rector's heart ?

At one time the two boys used to " read " at the Rectory, and the reverend tutor strove to hold the scales of justice with a severely

even hand; and yet was it not a fact that
Master Cyril got a thought more (unconscious)
help from the teacher, and was a thought
more tenderly dealt with in the matter of
fault-finding? Lance, with his dark, manly
beauty, and his close, determined ways, was
attractive in his own way; but it was not
Cyril's way—it had not Cyril's winsome, irresistible charm.

But we must describe the Rectory; it is
a great thing in a story to know your places
as well as your people, your frame as well as
your picture.

Round two sides of the garden (a very
monster of a garden) ran privet hedges—
hedges so thick and massive from years and
years of clipping and snipping, that they
looked as if you might almost drive a coach
and six along their broad, green, level tops;
and birds had long since given them up in
despair as possible building-places. Below
this hedge came a deep fall of the greenest,
softest turf, cut opposite the gates into steps
paved with white and shiny cobblestones.

The house was one of those delightful old
buildings that are all gables, and made a
perfect paradise for pigeons, who strutted,
pouted, cooed, or pirouetted, as it suited their
fancies, on the combs of those red gables, or
above the broad eaves that overlooked the
garden. There was one pigeon with such a
mighty tail, that when he stood on one leg
and spread it to the sun, he looked like an
opera-dancer *posée*, if such an enormity as a
coryphée on the roof of a sober clerical abode
can be even hinted at. Another had such
an enormous out-standing throat that he had
no small difficulty in looking over it, and
enjoying the fine prospect from the gable-
end as he should. White and black, grey
and pied, the pretty creatures would walk
gingerly down the inclined plane of red tiles
to their dovecotes, or sometimes, if the wind
was high, were blown ignominiously askew,
and had to put on an air of extra dignity
to make up for it when they reached the
natty little shelf before their round house
doors. Sometimes, too, the western sun

would shine upon the red, red tiles, and
between the two such a lovely glowing light
was born, that the pigeons looked like glori-
fied birds with ruby wings and golden throats;
and the Rector's daughter would clap her
hands, and cry to some one hidden somewhere out of sight—"Are they not dear
and lovely, those sun-bathed pigeons on the
roof?"

Now we come to one of the pleasantest
bits in our story.

The Rector's daughter — neither like an
angel, nor a sylph, nor a fairy princess, nor
any of those well-worn similes, but just the
bonniest, sweetest, fairest specimen of a young
English maiden—standing happy and elate
on the very threshold of womanhood, looking
at life, and all its exquisite possibilities to
come, out of eyes as blue as the violets that
lurked in the shadow of the wide privet
hedges round her father's garden—eyes set
in a delicately tinted face, that had a softened
resemblance to the lines of the Rector's own,
but with a little cleft (some people said pert)

chin, got from the pretty mother, who was now something of a chronic invalid, and whom father and daughter alike combined to pet and spoil, and compass about with the sweet and tender service of watchful eye and willing hand.

It was a matter of taste whether Alison Darling (she was called Alison after her mother's family, there being no male representative of the old stock left) was "sweeter and completer" with her sunny brown hair (more sunny, perhaps, than brown, yet with a hint of leaves in autumn too) falling in soft, rippling curls about her broad white brow, and lifted in a classic knot high on the top of her shapely head, or looking at you from under the shadow of a broad black lace hat, with a posy of pale pink roses set just above the brim, that formed such a pretty penthouse for the soft deep eyes and level brows. Her figure was graceful, yet gave you no idea either of attenuation or compression, but swayed easily from the pliant waist, while the generous shoulders

and rather full bosom told of perfect health
and vigour—a fact that was easily proved
by the many miles her tidy feet would carry
her through field and wood by the side of
the hearty Rector, who looked upon walking
exercise as part of the whole duty of man.
They were no silent companions these two;
indeed, you might occasionally hear them a
field or so off, the ripple of the girl's laughter,
the cheery tones of the father, making the
sun-bright world about them all the brighter.

On the side of the Rectory garden that was
not privet hedge was the great poultry-run.
It was built up against the wall of the stables
and outhouses, and had a roof like that of
a Swiss châlet, but the inhabitants thereof
enjoyed perfect liberty, roaming about at
their own sweet will and pleasure outside the
garden, and only retiring to their demesne
when the sun fell low, and the shadows
stretched across the emerald-green carpet of
the Rectory lawn.

All the chickens were of the same breed—
grey-coated, with vandyke collars of silver

pencilling. There might be seen chickens big and chickens little, chickens fat and chickens slender, and two rival lords of the harem crowing lustily the one against the other, as if life depended upon victory.

What a sight it was to see the Rector's daughter, with her hands full of golden grain, standing on the lowest of the white steps outside the gate, and at her feet, and all around her, a struggling, clucking, scrambling mass of feathers!

With her neat grey dress fitting as only a well-made woman's dress can fit, and a bit of delicate creamy lace at her throat, she matches the chickens to a nicety, and as she makes pretty noises with her lips, and holds out her white helpful-looking hands, the birds become possessed by a perfect frenzy, and one bolder than the rest, and a bit of a favourite, too, it is to be feared—for favouritism, alas! is found in all classes of society—lights with a sudden rush of wings upon her wrist, and shoves his venturesome beak into her closed palm.

The picture is perfect.

Then there is the rose-garden. It is behind the house, and is a very nest of blossoms in summertide. It is not an ordinary rose-garden by any means, for Alison is ingenious as well as tasteful, and so there are posts set at distances all round it, and slender chains swing from one to the other. Round these the climbing roses have flung their bud-gemmed branches, and at their own sweet will have woven garlands, in which Titania might love to sway beneath the moon, and her elves to play hide and seek in.

At one side the lichen-covered wall formed a sort of grotto with a shallow-arched roof, and within ran a low broad seat, with a tiny table, just big enough to hold a lady's work-basket or a tray and tea-cup. Never was a snugger retreat or a more delicately fragrant one than the grotto in the rose-garden; for the roses were of that old-fashioned, pink-faced kind that exhale the sweetest breath, the veritable essence of attar, and, like a kind friend who helps another in making his house beautiful, a sweetbriar grew "all convenient-like," as the Rector's handy-man, Jonathan Straw, observed, just within reach.

But Jonathan must not be passed over with so casual a mention as this. He was no ordinary man, was Jonathan; neither in the estimation of himself, nor yet of any other man in Scarsdale Upper or Scarsdale Lower. There was nothing he could not "put his hand to," so to speak; nothing he would have been afraid to undertake.

Railways were a thing unknown in Scarsdale in this the year of our Lord 1857, and it may even be suggested that an omnibus would have been looked upon as a "new-fangled" kind of thing, whose trustworthiness could but be a matter of speculation even to the stoutest-hearted. Jollick's waggon was the stay of all right-minded persons who set out with stolid determination on an eight-hours' drive to York, for they felt that by using this time-honoured vehicle they were fulfilling a sacred duty to themselves and their families, and taking every possible precaution.

Jollick's waggon (or Jollick's, as it was called for short) was drawn by four grand horses with flowing manes cunningly plaited and adorned with many-coloured ribbons. Behind rode the guard, a small wizened chap, with a most unmelodious horn, on which he played with great content to himself and very little to other people. Jollick's ran to a country town about fifteen miles off, and then on to York, making the journey twice a week, running from and coming to the Golden Crown, that picturesque hostelry at the head of the village proper, where a crown, that must have been a Marquis's at least, was held forth by a stalwart hand and arm, and looked upon as a work of the highest and truest art.

Need it be said that the starting and arriving of Jollick's were events of no mean importance in Scarsdale? If you had done your day's work, and felt a little languid or low in your mind, you sauntered off with your hands in your pockets, and stood in front of the Golden Crown to watch for Jollick's.

Right opposite the inn, in a round, clear space where waggons and traps of all kinds used to turn, stood a wide and spreading oak, round whose goodly girth ran a circular wooden bench, and here a sort of village parliament would assemble on summer evenings, and, as the smoke from many pipes rose in curls of faint blue mist, all subjects of local dispute were sat upon, thrashed out, and dissected.

"It wur spoke on at t' oak-tree, I tell yo'," was a not infrequent phrase in Scarsdale, when the importance of some event was insisted on.

It was very bad for the name and fame of a village belle if she were "hard spoke on at t' oak-tree," and a scolding wife had been known—so it was said—to strive and mend her ways after passing through the same fiery ordeal.

Jollick's was about the size of a room, and could hold more parcels than any known vehicle since Noah's ark, which one would suppose must have contained a good deal of

luggage, as well as a fair show of live stock.
To stand by and watch the disembowelling
of this mighty van was indeed a pleasure
not to be despised, to say nothing of the
exquisite delight of afterwards commenting
on the extravagant purchases of this or that
neighbour — a comment accompanied by a
pious hope that he was "able to pay for
'em," and "knew his own business." It was
no manner of use, if you lived in Scarsdale,
Upper or Lower, to hope to buy anything
"unbeknownst," as Jonathan Straw called it,
because the local shops were strictly limited
to the plainest necessaries of life, and if you
went in for anything "extra fine," it had
to come by Jollick's, and the village parliament had to be allowed to see it unpacked.

Well, on one occasion, the driver of Jollick's
took it into his head at the very last moment,
when the four horses were tossing their be-
ribboned manes in impatience, and whisking
their heavy tails like so many threshing-
machines, to have some sort of a fit—a kind
of daze that called for such stringent measures

as being laid on his back on the stones of
the stable-yard, and having water poured over
his head, and brandy down his throat. There
stood Jollick's all ready to start, and everybody
was looking at everybody else to know what
was to be done, when up stepped Jonathan
Straw, one flower stuck in his bosom, another
in his hat, and a perky smirk upon his face.

"Give us the ribbons, Sam," he said to an
attendant ostler, and up he climbed on to the
high box-seat, crack went the whip, twang
went the horn, and Jollick's, driven by the
Rector's handy-man, was out of sight in "two
ticks of a lamb's tail," as Sam graphically
put it.

"Bless my soul!" said the Rector when
told of the disappearance of his factotum,
"that man would lead an army into battle at
a moment's notice, and look as if he had been
born in a red-coat and carried a sword from
his infancy."

As for Alison, she walked down the village
next evening to see Jollick's come in, and
the "whip-salute" that Jonathan gave her,

and the great, glad smile that overspread his face at sight of her, were things to be remembered.

But " Maister Straw " was not only a Jehu ; time could not stale his infinite variety—not it, or, as the village put it, " You never knew when you had him." On Sundays he constituted himself a sort of supplementary apparitor, and, as a matter of course, appeared at Sunday-school, and occasionally in the vestry to assist in robing the clergy. This last office he did in defiance of one Pilkington, the properly constituted parish-clerk (whose masterly rendering of the responses was reported to have a more than merely local fame), and in spite of the said Pilkington glaring at him mildly, did manipulate surplices (cassocks were things unknown in those unenlightened days), handle stoles, overturn hassocks in an indiscreet eagerness, and ingratiate himself with the reigning curate, whoever that potentate might chance to be. One story of Maister Straw is too good to be passed over in silence.

The predecessor of the somewhat feeble
Mr. Westerton had been a certain Mr. Ullathorne, a manly, independent sort of young
fellow, too straightforward himself to suspect
design in others, and engaged to a woman
whom he dearly loved, and was only waiting to marry until preferment should shine
upon him.

Mr. Ullathorne was striking-looking in
appearance, and peculiarly striking in the
cricket-field, where his hitting powers struck
terror into the elevens of the adjacent villages ;
he was quickly popular with the inhabitants
of Higher and Lower Scarsdale, and, alas !
painfully so with the younger ladies of the
congregation, married and single.   The former
aspired to be his chosen friends, and to make
him their Protestant   father-confessor ; the
latter aspired—heaven only knows where their
aspirations ended !

With the ready intuition of the rustic mind,
Maister Straw grasped the whole situation—
the ladies' ardour, the curate's unsuspicious
nature.   True, it struck the latter as rather

odd that Mrs. This and Miss That should so
often meet him after Sunday-school, just at
the turn that led to his lodgings, and that they
should take such an interest in the view from
the churchyard after evening service. But
his mind was clear as shining water, and he
held to the old-fashioned idea that if a man
wanted to seek a woman out, either as friend
or lover, he could do so without her flinging
herself at his face or into his arms, as the case
might be.

However, his eyes were shortly to be en-
lightened and his mind expanded.

"Bide a bit, sir; bide a bit," said Jonathan
Straw to him one evening after service, edging
in between the curate and the vestry door.
"Not yet, sir; not yet. It isna safe."

"Safe!" echoed Mr. Ullathorne, in an
amazed tone of voice, taking a step backward
as though he were afraid the self-constituted
apparitor had been dallying injudiciously at
the Golden Crown, and was in the stage called
"seeing rats." "Safe, my good man; what
do you mean?"

Straw edged close up, and spoke in a blood-curdling whisper—

"The lions are in the path, sir."

There was a long pause, and then an amused smile broke over the face of the curate. His eyes were no longer holden; he took in the position fully; and being wary as well as brave, laid down for himself from that very hour such a line of conduct as completely routed the enemy.

Of course his popularity with the upper ten of the congregation suffered, and Miss Medlicott, the local solicitor's daughter, avowed that she considered he had been "greatly overrated"—an opinion that was ratified by a sort of female Greek chorus on the spot.

Mr. Ullathorne only stopped long enough to win all one season's matches for the club. Then preferment came, and, heartily regretted by the working population and by the family at the Rectory, the old curate departed, and the new man reigned in his stead.

Mr. Westerton was a tall, slim young man, with a long nose, large, near-sighted eyes, a loose-lipped mouth, a confidential manner, and a vanity gigantic in its proportions. He was the son of an old college friend of the Rector, or very shortly after his first appearance on the horizon he might have required a return-ticket for Jollick's. As it was, he was conscientiously made the best of by the Rector, Mrs. Darling, and Alison, and petted—of course metaphorically and in the strictest propriety—by the "lions" already alluded to.

"Don't talk to me," said Jonathan to the village conclave. "He's a reg'lar sawney, is t' new parson; and as for them lions, as goes about seekin' whom they may devour, as Scripter hath it—why, he's a very Daniel among 'em, so he is."

Some confusion must have existed in the good man's mind as to the circumstances under which the prophet came into the gruesome assemblage in the rocky den; but, notwithstanding, the hit told, and was passed on from one to the other as "Maister Straw's lattermost sayin'."

However, the lions were delighted, and all the more so because it became presently manifest that Mr. Westerton did not admire Alison Darling. Now Mr. Ullathorne had been culpably outspoken on the subject, and was reported to have said openly that he looked upon her as "a noble type of woman."

"Not a very nice remark for an engaged man, I must say," said young Mrs. Mandeville, with a sniff.

Mr. Westerton gave a kind of feeble mental kick.

"Well, I don't know; a man can't be expected to go through life with his eyes shut just because he is engaged, you know."

But they "didn't" know. They were very severe, and in the end Mr. Westerton had to make an uncomfortable meal off his own words.

"Then, such a name for a young girl!"

"Darling!" said Miss Medlicott, who acted as walking-stick to Mrs. Mandeville, covering her platonic flirtations, as it were, with a

decent mantle, and picking up such crumbs
of comfort and attention as came in her way.
"I'm sure if I had such a name I should
blush every time I heard it."

"Still," said Mr. Westerton, meekly just,
"she can't help that, you know, and the
Darlings are a very old family."

They said how kind he was, and how good-
natured, at which he smiled naïvely. Thus
in moments of weak disloyalty, resulting from
the flattering and fluttering attentions of silly
women, did the Rev. Sleeksby Westerton fall
so low as to belittle those whom he knew in
his heart of hearts to be as far above their
detractors as the stars are above the earth.
Thus did he wander (accompanied by syrens)
about the sun-touched meadows and down
the ferny lanes, knowing that two pages only
of his sermon of Sunday had been wrestled
with, and that the sick and sorrowful were
needing comfort; knowing that he ought to
be about his Master's business, instead of
dallying in the dales eating thistles.

Mr. Westerton was very fond of preaching;

indeed, being but a foolish young man at best, it was about the only chance he had of getting any sensible people to listen to him. True, the Mandevilles, Medlicotts, and other ornaments of the parish declared he had a voice "like a sacred flute," whatever that instrument might be, and several precious extracts from his discourses were transferred to diaries that closed with little impregnable locks; but beneath the scum of folly on the surface a longing for better things lurked in the recesses of the curate's nature, and this better self of his was fully capable of setting down such popularity at its true worth.

Even while he cheapened the Rector's daughter, he knew that to hear her clear, sweet voice say, in that frank outspoken manner that clothed her about as a gracious garment, "Well done! well done!" would have been to him like the new wine that is said to strengthen man's heart and make him of a cheerful countenance.

Perhaps we have lingered somewhat long with Mr. Westerton, but he has his little part

to play in this our story, and it is as well
to see him clearly with our "mind's eye,"
ere progressing with the thread that seems
inclined to become slightly entangled and
twisted.

CHAPTER IV.

ONE or two touches are still wanting to complete the portrait of the Rector of Scarsdale. He must of necessity be a grand and noble figure on our canvas, but there are delicious sidelights, little gleams and glints of humour about him that have not yet been put in. There was not that twinkle deep down in his kindly eyes for nothing; witness a certain occasion called by common consent "Wake-'em-up-Sunday," which gave food for discussion to the parliament under the oak for many a day—nay, year—to come; for, like some amphibious bird that dives and dives, and then suddenly appears on the surface again, "Wake-em-up-Sunday" would sink into apparent oblivion; and then suddenly, on the appearance of a newcomer, the story had to be told all over again, with those little addenda that gather and adhere to an oft-told tale as snow to the rolling ball. It may be that Mr. Westerton's rounded periods and delicate similes were too scholarly—a bit what is called "over the people's heads;" at all events, the people's heads (that is, the common people's) began to nod, more especially at afternoon service; and, as nodding is infectious, the ailment spread, and it came about (this being summer-time) that slumberers were many among the Scarsdale congregation, and a scandal to the church was threatened.

Therefore, on one pleasant sunny afternoon, when the birds outside were twittering in the trees, and the drifting shadows of the fleecy clouds playing hide-and-seek among the tombstones, instead of the sonorous voice of their chief pastor greeting them as "Dearly beloved," lo! the slim curate set to piping the service, that "sacred flute," his high-pitched monotone, making unaccustomed music in the ears of his devotees. Then came the sermon; the text—"Therefore let us not sleep."

If there had been a gleam of humour in the good Rector's eye as he wrote that stirring discourse—a glimmer like the reflection of a dancing sunbeam in clear water—there was nothing but the most edifying gravity to be read in both look and voice as he gave out his text—"significant of much."

"Therefore let us not sleep."

How they sat up, jerking and preening themselves, as it were! How rustic elbows nudged rustic sides, and the more habitually wakeful looked reproachfully at acknowledged sinners! How drooping heads became erect with a jerk; sleepy eyes bright and as wide awake as it was possible for eyes to be! What a study of human nature was provided by that most uneasy congregation!

One woman, whose soporific spouse appeared to be proof against all appeal, after trying in vain every dodge possible and impossible to rouse him to a full sense of his position, melted piteously into a silent flow of tears, furtively wiping away the tell-tale drops with the end of her bonnet-strings.

"Therefore let us not sleep."

The discourse moved serenely on — the duty, the blessings of activity, the industry of daily life, industry in the smallest things, as well as in the greatest—a sermon to catch and hold the attention of just such a congregation as were gathered together to hear it.

But the Scarsdalians knew what was coming; they might have said, "By the pricking of 'our' thumbs, something wicked this way comes."

And at last it came.

The beauty and gift of sleep—sleep that rests the weary brain and restores the tired-out body—sleep, the gift of God. "He giveth His beloved sleep." Like any other good gift, sleep was liable to abuse.

Here came a sort of rustling sound, like the stirring of a breeze among the leaves of a forest.

The sin of sloth—the lazy, laggard habit of body and mind—sleep that was "not con-

venient," that was a hindrance and bad example to others.

Illustration of this—

The kindly host bidding his friends to
his house; the loving welcome that awaits
them : the poor appreciation of that welcome
shown by some. . . .

Here the rustling sound was again audible,
and significant looks passed from one to the
other.

It will be easy for any one to follow out
for themselves the concluding application of
the Rector's sermon on "Wake-em-up Sunday;" to imagine the crush of members of
the village-club round the oak-tree that night,
the Babel of tongues, the conflicting opinions,
the wise saws, the advice gratis, the exultation of the righteous, the confusion of known
sinners.

To say his say, deliver his blow to right or
left, and then carefully to abstain from discussion, this was the Rev. Mr. Darling's way
with his people ; hence he might never have
known the extent of the sensation caused by

"Wake-em-up Sunday," but for Danny Spool.
In that great and coming country Australia,
they have a delicious word for describing a
little Jack-of-all-trades : they call him the
"knock-about-boy."

Spool was the knock-about-boy of Scarsdale
village.　If he had lived in a city—say Paris,
by way of suggestion—he would have been a
second Gavroche.　He was quick-witted, agile,
"slape as a foumart," as Jonathan Straw ex-
pressed it (that is, "slippery as a weasel"),
and possessed a stock of native impudence
that might have set up, say, a round dozen
other boys, and still left a margin of goods
to spare.

He lived with his maternal grandam, one
old Mother Bond, who bore a somewhat
shady reputation as being of witch-like
tendencies and secretive habits, and the
sight of whose bent form and eerie elf-locks
of grey unkempt hair floating about a face
like a withered apple stale with keeping,
might have been picturesque, but was certainly not inspiriting.　He lived, that is, he

ran home at night to his small bed under the sloping thatched roof of her diminutive cottage down below the Meadows.

In these days Danny Spool would have been caught and winged by the School Board, and proving contumacious, would have been despatched to a reformatory. But in the time of which we write, such wholesome restraints upon the overflowing spirits of the rising generation were not in vogue, and all the educational advantages enjoyed by Spool were certain forcible appearances at the dame's school below the church, attended by various escapes from the same, mostly made through the window while the worthy dame's back was towards the culprit.

"You might as well try to catch a boggart," said Master Straw.

But Spool had his good points. His grimy fingers were marvellously skilful; his ten-year-old brain more cunning than many of forty. He was "knowledgeable," the folks said, and knowledgeable is a word that means

a good deal. Never was such a hand at
weeding as Spool. The weeds disappeared as
if by magic, and many a day's work did the
lad get in the Rectory garden or about the
premises.

For the Rector's daughter this strange wild
freak of Nature had the unreasoning devotion
of a dog. He would follow, fetch, and carry
for Miss Alison as willingly as though her
purchased slave; he would do anything for
her—except learn the letters of the alphabet.
This desirable state of things Alison set herself to try and bring about. She purchased
a book with letters therein inscribed almost
as big as Spool himself; she ordered him to
wash his hands and face and put on his best
clothes—such a best!—and present himself
every Saturday evening before her.

This he did gladly; seated himself at the
highly-scrubbed table in what she called her
"village-room," a tiny apartment built out
from the house, and used for parish purposes,
and Alison began.

She prided herself on being a good teacher,

and was, indeed, inexhaustible in patience.
She endeavoured to make those signs and
symbols that enable us to express our thoughts
on paper as interesting as possible, illustrat-
ing great A by an actual apple, which Spool
promptly pocketed, laboriously buttoning up
his trousers-pocket for its greater safety. She
went on explaining—dear hopeful soul !—and
was glad at last to feel intuitively that her
little pupil was interested, and wanted to
"ask a question," as the Sunday-school children were in the habit of putting it, when
prompted to interrogate the teacher on some
abstruse theological item.

She turned to him with an expectant
smile.

"What's yon ?" said Spool, pointing with
a newly, but imperfectly, washed finger, to a
stuffed bird of foreign origin that in a glass
case adorned the wall over the mantelshelf.
"Wha' shot 'un ? Wur it t' parson ? He's
a gradely soart, ony way."

Nature was Spool's book; the birds and
beasts and fishes therein to be found, the

letters of his alphabet. Whispers as to the boy having gipsy blood in him were not unknown in Scarsdale, but had of necessity to be furtive, lest, coming to the ears of Mother Bond, they might be taken as an insult, and straightway the offender's horse should fall lame, or his cow die in calving, events not unknown to have happened— according to popular belief—when the recluse of the wood below the meadows had been offended.

Spool also had his trials.

Poor Benedict tells us that the only rhyme he can find for "lady" is "baby," and for the name of Spool the rhyme was so offensively obvious, that even the least gifted village-poet could make infinite variations in its possibilities.

"If I'd er know'd it, I'd er ketched on to some other name," said the "knock-about boy" aggrievedly to Alison; "an' there's nothin' of the fool about me when you come to that."

Which was more than true, for his escapades

by field and flood, his poachings on Sir Marmaduke Peyton's preserves, his purloining
of loose horses, and long rides taken at day-
break—at that early hour when the birds
begin to sing matins, and the little rabbits
wake and skip—these were not the adventures
of a fool, but rather of some tricksy spirit,
like to the little "ground men" of the fairy-
tales.

There was one house in the dual village
that Spool ever gave a wide berth to; as
well he might, for, written over the door in
stout, if somewhat straggling letters, was the
following ghastly announcement:—"A constable lives here."

That "a" constable was also "the" constable
—in fact, that there was no other representative of the law nearer than the country
town to which Jollick's was won't to convey
any offender who might be guilty of serious
misdemeanour, made no difference to the
awe-inspiring nature of the said announcement. The sight of the constable himself—
an inflated and blusterous Dogberry, as indeed

became his office—looking through a small
side-window alongside the door (popularly supposed to have been constructed for the express
purpose of that functionary keeping an eye
on all the wickedness of the world without)
was enough at any time to give the smaller
children of the village fits.

But Spool, keeping, however, a respectful
distance from the actual abode of the enemy,
would greatly haunt and distress the footsteps
of this potentate, bringing to him vain and
idle complaints, and mythical yet disturbing
tales of poachers heard or seen in the Peyton
preserves. Looking upon the gamekeeper of
those lands as a hated rival, the constable
would carry these fabulous stories to him
with unction, as being an arm of the law
whose zeal ran far ahead of that of the other;
but on several occasions the only result of
all this was that the keeper wrung the ear
of Spool next time the two met, and sent
him shrieking to Mother Bond. Then the
keeper's wife would come to the fore, weep
bitter tears over her youngest born, and cry

aloud that if the sweet child grew up with
a bandy leg or a squint eye, it would be
"t' fayther's fault, for vexin' t' ould witch
and meddlin' wi' t' kid," which was hard on
the keeper, and only one more proof of what
all history tells us—namely, the fact that
superstition can back up the weakest cause,
and make it a terror to men.

Anyhow, the "kid," otherwise Danny
Spool, many times and oft got off scot-free
when his iniquities were such as to deserve
the severest measures. When annoyed by
Farmer Wringer over a little matter of tres-
pass, did he not climb the tall walnut-tree
in the field of the aggrieved party, and there
lurk with a patience past the telling? And
the good farmer passing in all good faith,
did not Spool shake the tree violently, saluting the enemy with a brisk and continued
fire of heavy ammunition? Mr. Wringer
naturally enough, looked up. to see whence
the shower of missiles came, and——

But let us draw a veil over the painful
scene, hinting only that as he strode, fuming

and swearing, home, he might very suitably
have indulged in a stave of the popular
ditty—

> " What a surprise !
> Two black eyes."

Of course he vowed vengeance against the
sinner (who had escaped during the temporary
blindness of the would-be pursuer) ; but alas !
Mrs. Wringer—then in a somewhat delicate
state of health—cried out, with tears, that
if he wanted to see her laid a " silent corpse "
in the churchyard, and " read over " by the
Rector in due form, a good way to bring
such a state of things about would be to
" persecute " Mother Bond's boy, and get a
" shadow " put on the farm and all in it.

What could the farmer do after that ?

Truly a very Puck was Danny Spool, and
happy the man who could put salt on his
tail, as the saying goes, and wing him for
once and for all.

But, then, he was so handy !

If any one was in a strait, wanting a job
of work done in a hurry, and with no one

to do it, why, there you were, you know! Rather, there was Daniel Spool at your service, limber, willing, elfish, quick of eye and light of hand.

The people of Scarsdale had proved it a thousand times, and the imp had acquired a sort of Mascott reputation. If you wanted to get your hay in before a thunderstorm should break, and spoil it, why, get Danny Spool to give a hand. He was a lucky boy, he was, as every one knew. If you wanted your potatoes to give a good yield, you got Spool to plant an odd one or two.

There is nothing so invaluable to the possessor as a reputation of this sort. One may read in history the use that mediæval saints made of such prestige.

Well, behold this "lucky boy" seated in a *dégagé* manner atop of a gate, his apology for a cap shoved to the back of his head, his trousers braced in graceful fashion just under his armpits, his legs bare from the knee, his toes—prehensile, like those of a chimpanzee—clinging fondly to the bars, his curly locks

and sly blue eyes giving him a certain pictur-
esqueness, and his *dents de jeune chien* displayed in a cheerful and somewhat patronising
smile—a pleasant figure enough to come upon
during a rustic stroll, and one that might
well have caught the eye of any wandering
artist.

Assuredly the "points" of the picture
struck the Rector forcibly as he came down
the adjacent lane, for the artist soul is im-
planted in many a breast, though the hand
may never wield brush or pencil.

Spool, catching sight of the tall, portly
figure all in black (in those days the clerical
fancy had not such wide fields to roam over
in the way of costume as is now held permissible), whipped off his scrap of a cap, and
dropped with equal grace and agility on to
his bare feet, standing at attention in a very
complete manner, but with a demure look
upon his elfin face that told of mischief lurk-
ing within.

"Good-morning, Danny," said the Rector,
with a cheerful smile.

"Mornin', sir," answered Danny, apparently trying to uproot the front curl of his well-covered pate, "an' it *be* a good mornin', too, yer worship, which wur just what I wur a-thinking to mysel' as you come along—good for taters, and good for beastises, and good for everythink."

It struck Mr. Darling that the boy had some object in prolonging the interview—in other words, that he was making talk to gain time; hence always quick to fancy help of some sort might be needed, he stood awhile, looking across the gate at the fair, wide meadow-lands, where the corn was waving like a golden sea, and the cloud-shadows chased one another like the eddies in a flood.

Yes, he was right; this poor waif and stray, whom not even his practised touch could tame, had some cause to plead, some—very possibly touching—appeal to make.

He would meet him half-way.

"Well, my boy," he said, "what is it? Have you anything to say to me? Ah! yes, I thought so," for Spool had drawn near to the

Rector, with solemn eyes raised to his kindly face.

" Please, sor, that wur a fine preachment of yourn, a gran' discoorse. It wur like stickin' forks into 'em, so it wur. They'll keep wake enoo now, no fear, Sunday arternoons."

The Rector put on an indifferent air, and hummed a tune to himself softly as he went on his way.

That impish boy should not see that he was startled by this original style of criticism, not he.

But yet ! "sticking forks into them ! " Well, well, fame takes many shapes. Mr. Darling, however, soon told the tale against himself, and Spool also told his little story as to how he had " given his mind to t' parson," and the saying about the forks was universally accepted as a " sharp " saying on the part of the knock-about boy.

Then in the matter of recovering the lost, who could equal Danny ?

There was the case of Samuel Grimshaw, farmer, who mislaid a sow and her squeaking litter. Such goods may seem difficult things to lose, but granted a night's start, and plentiful expanse of wood and dale, and it is wonderful what a pig will do.

They sought her high, they sought her low, but the lady and her promising family were not to be found.

Old Grimshaw, being only a farmer in a very small way, was in despair, and, it was averred, sat down and cried on his own doorstep. However, next morning at the break of day his ears were assailed by sounds sweeter to him than the lilting of any nightingale.

A grunt, many squeaks, and a high, gleeful voice uttering various inarticulate sounds, supposed to be seductive to pigs, caused Grimshaw to rush out at his front gate, as his wife said, "like mad."

There he beheld Spool, waving his thin arms like a semaphore, and driving before him the lop-eared sow, her face caked with river-mud up to the eyes, and her curly-tailed, pink-skinned piglets frisking round like so many lambs in spring-time.

"He whistled to 'em," said the wiseacres, "and they had to coom."

"Loike enoo' 't ould woman sent 'em astray to get credit for the kid," surmised one, who was of a suspicious spirit.

Then, to turn to more aristocratic surroundings, just at the time our story opens, there was the well-known case of the peahen at the Old Hall.

Was not Mrs. Dutton, the housekeeper, half "out of herself" at the fact that the said peahen had betaken herself to the woods, and, as was surmised, there found some sequestered nook, laid a nestful of eggs, and become a happy mother? Every one knew of Mrs. Dutton's devotion to the peacock and his domestic circle. She explained to all comers that the loss of this particular peahen was the greater trial to her because she had reared it up "from a chick," leaving the listener to suppose that she might have reared it up from anything else if she had liked, but that, under such circumstances, it would not have been so admirable a specimen of its tribe.

But her mourning was turned to joy when Danny Spool appeared, chasing warily before him the missing matron, while the plaintive, melancholy "chee-eep" of five tiny creatures —some of them destined to wear arched tails full of eyes in the future, but not looking very much like it now—came from the rustling grass. The peahen kept giving out a harsh guttural note of call, now and again varied by a noise as though a rusty hinge creaked its loudest, and Danny Spool was singing high and shrill—

> "Old Danny Spool
> Is a silly little fool,
> And wunna go to sch . . . ule."

The exigencies of rhyme dominated the orthography, but this license has been claimed by the poets of all ages. Spool went round by what is called the "field-way" to the Old Hall, and so avoided any possible encounter with Sir Marmaduke, a personage to whom he gave at all times the widest possible margin, as knowing him to be far above the reach of superstitious influences, and credence in "lucky boys" who knew the whereabouts of every hare's "form," and the nesting-places of the pheasant and the partridge.

But herein Danny Spool was wrong. The tyranny of superstition was not unknown to the lord of the Hall, but, like most people, he had his pet superstitions, though these did not extend to Mascotts.

At sound of the knock-about boy's song out rushed Mrs. Dutton, cap-streamers flying, hands extended, a couple of attendant and obsequious housemaids in her train; and, by the united efforts of the lot—efforts slow and dignified on the part of Mrs. Dutton, like the movements of a sloop in full-sail—the peahen was safely lodged in an empty out-house, with "all her pretty ones," save one, safe and snug beneath her tender breast, the exception perching himself upon her back, and watching the general public with bold bright eyes from that fair vantage-ground.

"Bet-cher-life he's a knowin' one. He'll carry a tail afore he's done," said Danny.

"Ay," said an ostler loitering near, "an' he's not the only knowin' 'un in Scarsdale."

Danny laughed, hugging himself as was his manner when amused.

> "'Old Danny Spool
> Is a silly little fool,
> And wunna go t' sch . . . ule.'

But you canna find your pigs and your turkeys wi'out him, for a' that; and he's a knowin' 'un he is, bet-cher-life."

The "knowin' 'un" was soon seated on a rail near the back-door of the Old Hall, engaged in discussing some toothsome bread-and-jam, gazed upon with much interest by various retainers of the household.

Danny Spool appeared to have an inborn objection to sit on chairs like other people; he would crouch like a dog or perch like a bird, but to demean himself as an ordinary human being seemed alien to him.

Swinging his leg as he ate his jam and bread, he yet found time to give a furtive

and alert glance round about. Something
was giving Spool the fidgets. At last, when
the other spectators had melted away by
degrees, and only himself and Mrs. Dutton
(who stretched a point in regard to her
attentions to Spool on account of the uncanny reputation he bore) were left, the cat
emerged from the bag.

"Be Maister Cyril anywheres round?" said
Spool, leaning perilously over from his perch,
and clinging with his toes to the lower rail.

"No," said Mrs. Dutton; "he's gone horse-
back-riding along with Mr. Lance, you know.
We're all sad and sorry here, as the saying
goes—sad and sorry over Mr. Cyril."

"Maister Cyril!   What of Maister Cyril?"

The jam-and-bread was drooping in a limp
hold; the muscles round Danny Spool's mouth
twitched.

"He's going for a soldier."

"Wheer?"

The one word came rather huskily, and the
remnant of bread-and-jam fell to the ground.

"Across the seas, to a far, far land," said

Mrs. Dutton, catching her breath like one about to break into sobs.

"To a far, far land!"

Danny's eyes seemed to be looking for that distant land—looking—looking to where the golden sky turned the firs on the hill behind the house to ebony, and the sun was setting in a blaze of glory.

After a while he got down slowly from his perch, shook himself together, and then, carrying his cap in his hands, and with a strange, bewildered look in his small, pinched face, took his way silently homewards.

That night Mother Bond went through strange and remarkably unpleasant experiences.

She loved her rest, lying curled up like a dog and snarling in her sleep. Spool had often watched her, and wondered what she was dreaming of when she ground her few remaining teeth and worked her hands on the tattered quilt. But this night—the night after his adventures with the peahen—the boy woke her up more than once, laying

his hand upon her shoulder and shaking her
gently from side to side.

It seemed that his loneliness was so great
he must have some one to speak to.

"Mother, he's going for to be a sodger in
a far, far land beyond the seas."

Then Mother Bond would eye the small
figure huddled together in the patch of
moonlight made by the high window in the
thatched roof — the desolate-looking little
figure, with its head upon its arms, and so
watching, fall to slumber again. At their
scanty breakfast next morning she heard
Danny mutter to himself the same words:
"Going for to be a sodger—going for to be
a sodger!"

We all make a mythology for ourselves.
In Danny Spool's there were two deities who
reigned supreme—the Rector's daughter and
Master Cyril at the Hall.

Once the boy had broken his leg (in no
very creditable adventure, you may be sure).
Alison had come to see him, braving Mother
Bond and the evil eye, had sat by his bed

—such a bed as it was—read to him, talked
to him, crooned over him ; and the young
master, the beautiful young master from the
Hall, whom everybody loved, he came too.
He brought bunches of grapes—some black
and some white—and soup in a little mug.
Indeed, it was a beautiful time for Danny
Spool, though his leg pained him so that the
tears would come stealing down his face
sometimes, and had to be wiped away with
a dirty little fist. Lying there under the
sloping roof, the boy constructed his mythology, with the result that has been already
mentioned.

When it was all over, he had to say something to Alison of what was in his heart.

"I'm not worth it, miss," he said. "I'm
a bad sort of a chap, you know. I'm not
worth it."

And now one of the gods of this mythology
of Danny Spool's was going "to a far country
beyond the seas," and he had to sit hunched
up in the moonlight to think about it, and
to go into the woods in the morning and

tell the birds and the squirrels about it, and
to listen to what the voice of the mill had
to say about it, and to hang on the bridge
and look deep down into the water rushing
through, and wonder if it ran on and on
and on until it got to the sea, and so on
and on again, till it washed the shores of
that far country to which Mr. Cyril was
going " for to be a sodger."

It was not often that Sir Marmaduke
passed through the village, but fate willed
that he should do so towards the evening of
the day after his son Cyril left the Old Hall,
and while the disappearance of Dorrington
was still fresh in his mind.

The action of this humble servitor fretted
Sir Marmaduke, as it were, to the bone. The
thought of it was like a gnawing pain. Could
he not buy a commission for his son and send
him to join his regiment in India but that
the servants of his household, without leave
or warning, must desert their posts and fly
the country?

The unacknowledged jealousy of the fair-haired boy—who had been for ever, so it seemed to his distorted mind, in his pathway —rose in its might, blinding his eyes, confusing his perceptions. Was he to vex him still, though with every moment that passed the watery space that separated him from his native land grew and grew, ever widening, ever spreading?

His wife's face—white and wan—with eyes that looked yet saw not what they looked on, but were ever gazing somewhere "far away, far away," ever seeking the lost boy —how he longed to fly where he could see no more its silent reproach, its unappeased hunger of the heart!

There is always comfort for the restless in the fresh air of heaven. We rush to Nature when humanity vexes us.

Sir Marmaduke that day roamed far over dale and hill, followed — ah! how generous and forgiving was the nature of that noble animal!—by Hound, keeping well to heel, and carrying his grand head droopingly,

as though still holding in his memory the
degradation of the night that was past, but
yet faithful; even giving tongue when a
tramp turned and looked after his master
with stolid curiosity.

Strangely enough, Sir Marmaduke came
through the village of Upper Scarsdale, and
so through the Meadows, passing on to the
spot where stood Mrs. Bond's ruinous cottage. Here was surely some unaccustomed
turmoil.

Hound stopped short and lifted his head
at the sound of a keening cry—a wail such
as some dumb animal in pain might utter;
and about the crazy door and in the bit of
weed-grown garden a little crowd had gathered
—people from the village and workers from
the mill.

Sir Marmaduke stopped short opposite the
gateway that had no gate.

"What is this outcry?" he said; and the
little crowd fell apart.

Upon the threshold of her sordid home
crouched Mother Bond, her white elf-locks

shrouding her face, her hands clasped about her knees.

"What ails the woman?" said Sir Marmaduke again, looking round about him as one who is not used to have his queries met with silence.

"Her boy, Danny Spool, him as she doted on—he's gone."

"Gone! Where?"

"Gone to be a sodger—same as Maister Cyril."

He turned about as though something had stung him.

Who dared to couple his son's name with that tatterdemalion, that good-for-naught, that graceless brat, Danny Spool?

But among so many it was hard to localise a voice.

"He's gone along wi' Jem Dorrington, Sir Marmadook," said another; "he wur breakin' his 'art, wur Danny, and he just up an' orf for to be a sodger, same as Maister Cyril."

At this Mother Bond peered from under her shaggy brows, rose slowly to her feet,

and so, swaying, held out her two arms
straight — each outstretched finger pointing
to the lord of the Old Hall.   Her head
wagged, and she muttered as one who weaves
a spell.   Then, as he passed on quickly up
the lane, her voice rose to a shriek—

"No son of thine shall live to fill thy
place.   No son of thine! no son of thine!"

The words rang out after him, and he
heard them; but he made straight on, never
once turning.

CHAPTER V.

THERE are sorrows that are implacable. They will exact the uttermost farthing of pain— pain that there is no glossing over, and for which no anæsthetic has ever been discovered.

Such a sorrow is a mother's for her son. Life and its duties cannot be put aside ; other trials, other joys, come and go ; but the ache of loss is lying there deep down in the riven heart. The wound never heals ; it is as hunger and thirst that nothing can satisfy or slake. To use the old imagery of the Valley of Hinnom, it is as the worm that never dies and the fire that is never quenched.

When the morning broke, and a new day began, it seemed to the mother of Cyril Peyton that her sorrow and her desolation met her like a pall, and that for her the very brightness of the sunshine was blotted out.

For lack of the sound of his step, for lack of the ring of his voice, all the world about her seemed to be filled with a cruel silence. A little trinket, a book, an old childish toy, the sight of these would stab her like a dart; she would kiss them all over, and then, laying them down, feel as though she had but newly parted from her darling. She was happy at times; but that was when she was dreaming. Sleep and darkness gave her back her boy. He came to meet her with his shining eyes fixed on hers, and his sweet lips smiling; she caught the glint of the sunshine on the glory of his hair; laughed in her dream to think she had been mad once, and fancied him far away; then woke to find that fancy was reality, and seeming false—woke to the bitterness of loss, yet dare not weep, lest her husband, sleeping in the room beyond, should hear, and, on the morrow, scourge her sick soul with hard reproaches as to the sin of idolatry, and compare her to the " stiff-necked

generation" whose rebellious spirit had called
down the curse of an offended God. A very
frenzy of protest would arise within her as
her husband hurled at her devoted head the
theory of universal depravity, reasoning that
on no "child of clay" should our affections
be set. The rigid Puritanism that bound him
down as withes might bind the body, slowly
destroying all power and deadening all healthy
impulse, incapacitated Sir Marmaduke Peyton
from fully realising the torture he inflicted,
and the daily sin of cruelty in which he lived.
The mother hungered for her son; and when
she would have craved some crumb of comfort, the hand that should have been her best
comfort gave her, in lieu of bread, a stone.

Lady Peyton had not expected—what sensible mother does?—to keep her son always;
but this loss, this sudden wrench had come
upon her so suddenly, with so little preparation, she was like one who, falling into sleep,
awakes maimed of a limb. She would always
go on, always try to help those about her,
always watch for the faintest, smallest sign

of the dawn of better things between her husband and herself, of a nearer sympathy, a closer, holier life; but she would go on as the lame may, with pain and effort, a halting creature who had lost a limb.

Lady Peyton had not married what is called very early in life—that is, not as some do, almost before girlhood has ripened into womanhood; hence it came about that now, with young sons, she was a woman of middle-age, while the hand of time began to plough its furrows in her husband's face, and whiten his clustering hair. Indeed, it was noted by many that the rippling braids of my lady's locks, just above the ears, began to silver from the day when Master Cyril sailed for foreign lands, though the erect carriage of her head and the noble dignity of her mien remained unchanged. Mothers in the openness of their hearts going to condole with her on parting with her son, meeting the anguish of her eyes, found themselves possessed with a dumb spirit, and could only stammer out an odd word or two of the sympathetic speeches they had had it in their hearts to make. Then would they hurry home in a flutter like ruffled hens, and, the haven of their own homes reached, enjoy the satisfaction of a "good cry," and seek relief in sudden letters or dispatches of plum-cake and pots of jam to hobbledehoys at school in various parts of the country, or in huggings and kissings of baby, during which process the bored infant was spasmodically assured that he should "never, never leave his own, own mussey, nor go across the naughty, naughty sea."

Your ordinary, common-place woman is much given to be taken that way before a silent sorrow that she cannot fathom — a passion that dwarfs her own common-place yet sincere emotions, and fills her with awe, as a dark, mysterious church, seen through a lifted curtain, affrights a child.

Of what avail, then, was it to this woman, whose heart was a mystery of pain to those about her, to be told that to mourn thus deeply for her boy was the greater sin, since

the "workings of grace" could not be discerned in that clear young soul? Did not
her heart cry out, "Give him back to me as
he is, with all his wayward ways, his happy
laughter, and his tender jesting—give him
back to me; my boy, my boy!"

Only the silence around her answered the
futile prayer. No bird's song in the larches
could delight her ear, no flower smell sweetly
in her nostrils.

She turned timidly, almost like a shy girl,
to Lance for comfort, but after a while a
creeping and sinister influence came between
the two so nearly drawn together.

For hours and hours Lance would be
closeted with his father in the library. Sometimes, as she passed the door, Lady Peyton
could hear the murmur of voices; one—so
it seemed — in expostulation; the other—
once, at all events--in sad, almost whining
entreaty.

Now and again the servants would come
to her, perplexed, and asking for counsel.
The library door was locked. What should

they do? The ordinary offices could not be performed.

For three people to live in a house together, while one is conscious of a secret and hostile understanding between the remaining two, is at all times a situation containing the most lamentable possibilities.

Lance had always been self-willed, arrogant, indifferent, selfish in his own small sphere; but how it was that he now became cringing, moody, morose in his ways, ready to start at any sudden noise or unexpected step? His mother was cruelly perplexed to understand all this. He seemed, too, to lose all pleasure in those manly sports in which he had always been a proficient.

When Cyril went away his horses were sold. This was a clear case enough, but those appropriated to the use of the elder brother followed, and that potentate Mr. Jennings began to wear a furtively anxious look, as though he feared for those "carriage bays" dear to his heart.

The Australian gladly secured these dis-

carded "cattle," known to be superior in
every point. He was educating his son in
all the learning of the schools; his eldest
daughter, a young woman with a face that
looked as if it had been carved out of wood
and then scrubbed with sandpaper, was coming
to the front as a mighty huntress before the
lords and ladies of the Riding, and was said
to look well on Cyril Peyton's favourite mare.
If you are to push your way onwards and
upwards towards a new social level, you must,
as Mrs. Dutton put it, "do something per-
spicuous." You are not enough of yourself,
like those born to the purple; you must make
way in matters extraneous; you must spend
money like water; you must make yourself
talked about—not scandalously, but as having
gifts. Miss Australia had made up her mind
to ride hard into the heart of the county;
also to be what she was pleased to call "outspoken"—that is, to say the rudest and
brusquest things in the most unexpected
manner—to startle people all round, in fact,
and thus attain to a certain sort of notoriety.

The taking of Sebastopol had closed the Crimean war as a subject of conversation among the county folks. Then came the red glare in the East—the horrible dawn of the story of the Indian Mutiny. Many had friends, many had relatives, out there where the terrible drama was enacted, and as the days and weeks, each with its bloody record, wore on, nothing else was talked of, thought of, prayed over. But that story, too, had now been told, even to the last closing chapter. Calm had followed on to that tossing storm of terror and indignation that shook the heart of England to its very centre. The general interest, so long concentrated on great and stirring national events, now spread itself out again in a sort of thin layer over local and minor topics.

One of these topics was the "retrenching" system that was evidently going on at the Peytons, and the chronic depression of Lady Peyton.

"If you want to know what I think," said the wooden-faced woman, as she deftly con-

trolled the caracoling of poor Cyril's mare,
"I think they're all cracked; that's about
the tune of it."

Some one said the above was a very sharp
remark, and another, a man from the barracks
at York, who said, "Yes, it was rather a
cutting observation," thought himself vastly
clever, and resolved to repeat the *bon mot* at
mess when he should return to the bosom of
his regiment.

The light of our lives goes out; we sit and
watch with blinding tears the embers of our
happiness smouldering into touch-paper, and
the world about us, with an engaging grin.
surmises that we are "cracked" more or less,
and quite beyond mending.

We are not likely to meet wooden-face
again, so may here say that she eventually
married a real live, though deplorably impe-
cunious lord. If the first kiss was something
like saluting a nutmeg-grater, he bore it like
a man, and as "bounce" was just beginning
to come into fashion, and the polish of a
bygone chivalry becoming slightly dim, her

ladyship was a great success, an excellent wife,
and in a certain hearty, bouncing way, a good
mother, which shows what a paying game it
is to mount the hill of social renown with a
firm, resolute, and undaunted step.

It could not be that Lady Peyton should
wade through a flood of deep sorrow without
the Rector being conscious of her suffering.
Perhaps she would have been startled if she
could have realised how thoroughly he grasped
it in all its bearings. The clinging to Lance
when Cyril was gone; the newly awakening
tenderness of the elder son; the pitiful clinging of the mother to a stay that proved, alas!
so frail and fleeting; the sinister influence
that withered and blighted this budding
flower of a sympathy in which some crumbs
of comfort might have been found, and then
the tired heart closing in again upon itself,
finding no consolation save in Heaven—all
these phases of a bitter sorrow were read like
an open book by the Rector's quiet observant
eyes.

Had there not indeed been a sad day of

parting at the Rectory when that bright boy
Cyril set out for foreign shores?

"I have passed the meridian of life," said
Mr. Darling to Alison; "I know not if I
shall ever see the lad again. We shall think
of him, shall we not, my dear, and miss him,
with his bright face and winning ways. Ah!
the young rogue, he often made a fool of me
in the old days, I fear."

Alison was grave and thoughtful, not even
the black fantail pirouetting on the roof with
more than his usual agility could win a look
from her, and none of the dogs (there were
many dogs at the Rectory) could win her into
a run round the garden and down by the rose
grotto—their favourite haunt. Here would
they spring elastic on to the wide stone bench
and all huddle up together, slyly endeavour-
ing to push one another off, while their young
mistress recovered her breath.

But no such gambols were found to be
practicable on the day of which it may well
be said it was a day of mourning.

How sad it all was!

The bright face that had ever been like sunshine among them, the merry tongue that had coaxed into smiles and laughter even the chronic sufferer on her sofa in the pretty chintz room that looked straight on to the vista of the long grass-laid walk that was always called "Mamma's Walk"—how these things would be missed!

In that quiet yet cheery chamber the comings of Cyril Peyton had ever been red-letter days. A woman's gentleness, a man's firm and helpful tenderness, the merry jest, the little thoughtful offering, these were the things Cyril brought to the sufferer.

"Cyril," said Mrs. Darling, as he bade her farewell, holding his hands in hers, while the tears fell thick and fast adown her thin, pale cheek, "who will make me laugh when you are gone?"

"Oh," he said lightly, yet feeling as short of breath as if he had just "got in" with half the opposing team at his heels, "I shall write you the drollest letters. I shall write often, and I shall never, never forget the

Rectory days, and all your goodness to me—never, dear Mrs. Darling."

He bent and kissed her.

Her tears blinded her, so that she did not see him go, but she heard his footfall along the hall; heard it stop; heard murmured words, and then the footsteps passing out and on into silence.

Alison and the Rector had waited for Cyril by the door. There had been a frank, brotherly kiss to the girl—a kiss as frankly returned as given—(fancy, if you can, the whites of Mrs. Mandeville's eyes, the shiver down the spine of dear Miss Medlicott, had they seen that innocent greeting)—a rather hoarse " God bless you, my dear, dear boy," from Mr. Darling, and Cyril Peyton was gone. No, not quite, for he stood a moment at the great white wooden gates that led into the lane, and made an upward gesture with his hand, as who should say, " I commend you to Heaven's keeping, for I myself may watch by you no more," and was gone.

I know that gesture well, always full of

the same sad significance—sometimes becoming clothed with all the hallowed sanctity
of a benediction by proving a supreme and
last farewell.

"My dear," said the Rector, as he and his
daughter turned into the house, "the autumn
is evidently close upon us; there is quite
a perceptible mist towards evening—ahem !
quite a perceptible mist."

"Yes, papa," said Alison.

Then the Rector took off his *pince-nez* and
wiped the glasses with deliberate care, walking slowly towards his wife's room as he did
so. She was in sorrow, he knew, and his
place was by her side.

It is not many men—no, not even the best
of them—who can stand chronic invalidism
in a woman ; but, of the few who can, the
Rev. Reginald Wentworth Darling was one ;
and perhaps the heaviest trial that could have
come to him would have been enforced
absence from this suffering wife of his when
she stood in need of his ministrations and his
tenderness. Her eyes were wet, her lips

tremulous as he took a chair beside her couch and laid his hand on hers.

"Wentworth," she said, "do you know what I was thinking of? 'There shall be no more sea.' I am sure that must mean no more parting; no more journeyings into a far country across great waters; no more watching the ship out of sight that carries your heart—your heart away with it. I am not thinking of myself—not chiefly, I mean —I am thinking of that poor mother—Cyril's mother."

"She has been in my thoughts and in my prayers all day," said the Rector; then he looked dreamily down the green alley, with its flower-pied borders on either hand, and murmured softly to himself: "No more sea —no more sea, and God shall wipe away all tears."

After that the two, husband and wife, kept silence, hand in hand, while the gloaming crept up over the flowers and along the velvety turf, hushing the birds to rest like the touch of a mother's hand.

Meanwhile Alison had gone quietly up to her own room—a very nest of a room—where in early summer the window, set deep in the wall, was hung round with the golden tassels of the laburnum that leant lovingly against the old house, and the chatter of the swallows under the eaves seemed to be close to your ear, and conducted in quite a confidential manner.

In the window was a wide, low, deep-cushioned seat, a favourite haunt with Alison, and close by it a small revolving bookcase, with all her favourite and best-loved companions set side by side and row upon row.

But to no well-loved book did she turn now. She sat her down in the green nook of the window, where the waning light filtered through the leaves, folded her hands in her lap, laid her head back against the wall of the curtained recess, and closed her eyes.

A favourite trick of Alison's this—a common habit. It was as though she wanted to withdraw herself from the world about her, and keep the silent company of her own thoughts.

"Having it out with things," she called it, and apparently the "having it out" was a complicated process on this occasion, for her pretty brows were knit, and at length a clear pearly teardrop stole from beneath her long lashes.

There was sorrow for the loss of her old playmate in Alison's heart, but there were other emotions too—fears for one dearer than life, apprehensions of she scarce knew what in the future; yet calming and stilling these a simple childlike faith—"my times are in Thy hands" —a faith without much profession perhaps, but deep as a clear mountain-lake, and as truly reflecting heaven.

For Lady Peyton, Alison had that almost worshipping love often called forth in a young girl by a woman many years her senior, but it was a worship constrained to silence by the very nature of the person upon whom it was bestowed.

What more simple, it may be said, than express the tenderness that lies in the heart? To have drawn that proudly-carried head

down to the resting-place of her shoulder, to
have touched the silvering hair with reverent
fingers, to have kissed the pallid, chiselled
brow, the white and tender hands—what
rapture!

Many times and oft had Alison done these
things in her fancy; in reality—though Lady
Peyton was dimly conscious that the girl's
heart was a full chalice, full of the red wine
of love, even to the brim, a chalice that her
lip might drain at will—no outward expressions of tenderness had ever passed between
them.

With a quickness born of keen intuition,
Alison also recognised that her father's sympathy with the lady of the Old Hall was one
to be felt, not spoken, and that its value and
its nature were understood and appreciated
by the one on whom it was bestowed.

She was, indeed, so near and yet so far,
this noble woman whose eyes were ever homes
of sorrow, and her lips set in the quiet lines
of patience and endurance.

Not even our nearest and dearest can help

us in the first heavy days of a great trial. The leaden-footed hours must drag along ; the waking from the sleep that cheats us; the shrinking, as from something that sears and burns, from familiar sights and sounds, now fraught with a bitter significance—all these must be met and faced as God shall give us strength, for man is powerless to help.

It may be said that Alison suffered for and with Lady Peyton in these days of darkness all the more because the longing to help and comfort must needs be stifled.

Lance, too, who had had a way of strolling down to the Rectory, loitering about the garden, watching the Rector tending and examining his various floral treasures, often with Spool as ardent and skilled assistant, or Master Straw, full of wise saws and confident suggestion — Lance was still absent, and Alison might have said with the heroine of the old song, "The village seems asleep or dead," so little do the presence of the many count with us when the one dearest of all is away.

For to Alison Darling the world centred a good deal in Launcelot Peyton, though as yet she hardly realised the force and passion latent in her own heart, and only awaiting the touch of a hand to arise in its might and fill her life even to overflowing. She only knew that whereas the music of her home-life had been always rhythmical and perfect, its chords of late had taken a higher, more piercingly sweet diapason; she only knew that the birds sang more clearly and with more jubilant note, the flowers gave out a more entrancing perfume, and even when the storm shook the branches and the rain beat hard against the panes, even then she could not quarrel with Nature, for such sweet thoughts kept her company, she never missed the sunshine.

A certain shamefaced feeling of guilt began to underlie her sweet service of love towards her mother, her ready help and sympathy in the Rector's daily cares.

Were these new thoughts of hers, that, like winged birds, all flew in one direction,

traitors to these dear guardians of her childhood and her beautiful, happy girlhood? She
even felt a craven before the grey, silver-
collared hens at times, and a Judas to the
favoured one who perched so confidingly on
her wrist and thrust his beak into her closed
hand for corn!

Was not her mind many times and oft,
quite in spite of herself, as it were, dwelling
in airy castles built by the shadowy hand
of Fancy — castles in which the dear old
home, with all its sights and sounds, and its
harmonies of love and tender service, found
no place?

There are times in a woman's life when
the very birds of the air, the very daisies
in the grass, seem to have eyes to read her
heart—for the thoughts and longings of that
heart to her fill all the world—and scarce
can she believe that what is so visible to
herself is hidden from others. It says much
of the home atmosphere at Scarsdale Rectory that Alison had never yet given one
serious thought to the fact of Lance being

Sir Marmaduke's eldest son and the heir to
lands and title. To her he was but her old
playfellow, so often in trouble over his books,
so often needing comfort. His dark, wilful,
passionate face had ever had a charm for
her, deeper than that of bright-faced Cyril.
Every one loved Cyril, few loved Lance;
hence Lance stood most in need of a supreme
and compensating devotion.

Thus argued the tender, woman's heart.
To be with Cyril pleased and delighted her;
his comings were as sunshine to the idolised
mother in her sick-room. But Lance—oh!
she longed for Lance to find comfort and
sympathy and solace in her presence; she
longed to be all and everything to him, to
make up to him for others that might look
upon him coldly! She would fain spend and
be spent on and for him.

We do not always open a book that lies
close at our elbows, and it may be said that,
so far, the Rector and his wife remained in
blissful ignorance of the idyll enacting before
their eyes. In truth, to them Alison was still

a child—the one child, as it were, in the universe; and to Mrs. Darling it seemed but as yesterday that she had sent for the then young Rector from his study, to witness the marvel of the little one's first staggering steps, feeling that no apology was needful even for interrupting the writing of Sunday's sermon under such a new and marvellous combination of circumstances.

It may be questioned whether Cyril had read his brother's heart, and knew of the yet unspoken love that had grown up from the childish companionship of past years. Lance was at all times reserved; Alison, for all her tenderness, proud, and one to hold herself thoroughly in check. Hence the play was played on silently, and with no audience. But this parting with Cyril tried the girl sorely; not only in the light of the loss of one dear to her as a brother, but because Lance and his mother must suffer, and she could do so little to comfort either. All common-places fail us when one who is infinitely precious to us is in sorrow. We feel the helplessness of ordinary words, and learn how dear the sufferer has grown from our own passionate longing to have the right of closer consolation.

It was pitiful to Alison to watch from a distance that in itself was cruel, the struggles of Lady Peyton to bear up bravely under the desolation that had come upon her. All the daily duties were taken up again after a while—a very little while—of inaction. One Sunday, and one only, the place in the Hall pew was vacant. Once, and once only, the weekly visitation to the sick in the village was omitted. Then routine, that pitiless wheel that revolves on and on and on, no matter how our hearts are riven or our eyes blinded with tears, took up the story of the days, and to the world around her the lady of the Manor was once more a familiar figure.

It so chanced that, wending her way to the scattered cottages beyond the Meadows, in one of which a child lay sick, Lady Peyton met Maister Straw. Now Jonathan was the most respectful of creatures, and never given

to putting himself forward, but on this occasion there was something strange about the
man. He had given an uneasy glance over
my Lady's head towards the bridge, and, as
she came up to him, brought himself what
he called "to anchor," pulling off his cap and
shifting uneasily from one leg to the other.

"Beggin' your parding, my Lady," said
Jonathan, "for bein' so bold, I'd take it
mighty kind if you'd call in one of these
days and see my old woman."

This was Jonathan's way of designating
his mother, with whom he still, being in a
state of single blessedness, kept house.

"Is your mother worse than usual? Is
there anything new amiss?" said Lady Peyton. "Surely I should have known; they
would have sent to the Hall."

When you only want to gain time, and
have in reality nothing to say, questions are
embarrassing.

But Jonathan was a man of resources.

"The haricot veins is still troublesome,
pertic'ler in one leg," he began.

But Lady Peyton interrupted him—

"That has been the case for five years past."

"True, your Ladyship; but they takes turns, does them legs of hers; and she's bin upset like. Yo' see, our neighbour, Sammy Holt, he went off terrible suddint. It wur wi' him same as Scripter hath it— 'When he woke in the mornin', behold he wur a dead corpse,' and them soart o' doings is terrible upsettin' to folks as lives handy."

"But Holt died nearly a year ago," said my Lady gently.

Jonathan's power of "makin' talk" had become exhausted; and yet he was determined not to pass on and leave "her Ladyships" until that weird, uncanny figure, now coming on behind straight from the mill-bridge, should have gone by and out of sight.

Suddenly a shrill and quavering voice broke into song—

> "Poor Danny Spool
> Is a silly little fool,
> An wunna go to sch . . . ule."

The last word, lingered on, rose to a

shriek that ended in a burst of cackling laughter, and then in a moment Mother Bond —for she it was—caught sight of the Lady of the Manor, and stood stock-still.

"It's Danny's grandam, your Ladyships," said Jonathan, all, as he subsequently declared, "in a twitter." "She's gone crazed-like of late, but she's harmless, and none of us likes to have her put by; some blight might come of it, you see, if she wur put by, my Lady."

Jonathan was almost whimpering in his abject apologies for the wild-looking figure standing there like the statue of one of the witches of whom we read in olden times, with her unkempt locks floating about her withered face, and her bare and skinny arms hanging by her sides. It is only to a chrysanthemum that it is given to be at once ragged and beautiful. Mother Bond was ragged, but she was not beautiful. To many she would have been repulsive. But there was no repulsion in Lady Peyton's quiet eyes as she gazed at the hag-like form in tattered, fluttering rags—the form that now

began to sway from side to side, uttering
a low, uncouth inarticulate cry inexpressibly
dreary in its desolate monotone.

"Poor soul!" said Lady Peyton, even
taking a step or two nearer to the uncanny
figure. "What has crazed her so? She was
a strange creature, but not like this. Has
anything happened in the village that I have
not been told?"

Jonathan subsequently, in the oak-tree
parliament, described his soul as feeling at
this moment "like a weaned child," but if
so, a weaned child must be a very uncomfortable kind of thing indeed, for Jonathan
was at his wits' end.

"It's the boy, your Ladyships; the boy
Danny Spool."

"Is he dead?" said my Lady, turning
her large, sad eyes on Jonathan so that he
squirmed again.

"No, no, my lady," stammered the troubled
"handy-man;" "he's gone away, is Danny;
gone for to be a sodger along wi'—wi'—
Maister Cyril."

Another moment and Mother Bond, the
crazy witch, was on her knees in the dust,
had caught my Lady's hand, and was mum-
bling and crying in a piteous, wailing little
litany of her own—

"He's gone, he's gone; my boy's gone
from me, same as your'n—same as your'n.
I shall never see him more—never no more,
never no more!"

"Well, well," said Jonathan, telling the
tale over and over to the village worthies
that night, "of all the imperence, puttin'
hersel' on a level, as you may say, wi' the
best o' quality, clutching her Ladyship's hand,
and a-kissin' of it! 'Jonathan, my boy,' says
I to mysel', 'you're a dreamin', you are,
that's about it. Bite yer tongue 'ard, and
that ull wake yer up.' But it wur no
dreamin' as was on me, neighbours; it wur
real, sound truth, and not tinkling symbols,
nor any such; an' I tell you, her Ladyship
spoke that gentle to that bewitched old
varmint, as it sounded like moosic played

soft on an 'arp, an' the tears come runnin'
over her face, and she said summat about
meetin' o' the boy in heaven, and there
should be no more sea, nor partin's, an' such-
like, and all tears should be wiped away.
And I arst you, neighbours, if it weren't
hard for a man to have to stan' by and
hear that young jackanapes as 'as stole my
bits o' apples, and played me monkey-tricks
enoo' times out o' mind, spoke of as a loikely
kind o' chap to be made a angel of one of
these fine days, to say nothin' of old Mother
Bond bein' there to meet 'im? Lord be good
to us, mates, but the ways o' quality is past
findin' out!"

CHAPTER VI.

JONATHAN STRAW MAKES A BET.

ON a certain Sunday afternoon, when the winter was what people call "breaking," and the birds were making little piping, uncertain calls from tree to tree, as much as to say, "Is it really true that spring is coming, comrades, and the warm, bright days are at hand?"—when the last snow had all melted from the corners of the steep church steps, and a faint pink tinge was stealing over the bare branches of the grand old trees seen from the churchyard, the Rev. Sleeksby Westerton displayed an unusual energy—one might almost say agitation—during his sermon, which was not lost upon his chosen followers and chosen admirers.

A "thrill," as Miss Medlicott put it, "shook her whole being." She was sure that some-

thing portentous had occurred.   She hoped it
was not sinful to be conscious of a longing for
the service to come to an end.

Presently, when some convenient oppor-
tunity should occur—Mrs. Mandeville and Mrs.
Barnstable-Ambler (a rather recent hanger-
on added to the group, and, alas ! a widow)
being out of the way—she would consult Mr.
Westerton as to the degree of sinfulness com-
prised in such a dereliction from duty, and
consult him as to the advisability of disturbing her family and distracting the servants of
the household by rising at an abnormal hour
for a week or so by way of penance.

Meanwhile she kept her bold black eyes
focussed to the face of the preacher ; listened,
as in a dream, to that sacred flute, his voice,
and waited, not unconscious that Mrs. Mandeville was fidgeting in her pew and letting off
her impatience by making her eldest hope—
a lanky girl of eight, who was always in the
way when she was not wanted, and suffered
from the peculiar, preternatural sharpness
called "long ears"—sit painfully upright and

still, while Mrs. Ambler became the victim of
a little nervous cough, and kept applying a
bottle of salts to her rather high nose.

If the three alert women could have looked
into the organ-gallery (which they could not)
they might have seen that Alison Darling,
her deft fingers pressing the music from the
ivory keys, was paler than her wont, and that
upon her lovely face was a look at once rapt
and sorrowful.

In blissful ignorance of anything unusual
in the atmosphere, the Rector read the service
in the simple, grand, emphatic way peculiar
to him.   Lady Peyton, the sole occupant of
the Hall pew, never raised her eyes from her
book.   At such times she was peculiarly alone
with the God in whom her trust was surely
stayed, in whom her confidence never failed.
"Even though He slay me, yet will I trust
Him," was ever the language of her heart.
The more lonely grew her life in the Old
Hall, the more she clung to the thought of
the life which is heavenly, the hope which
is eternal.   The petty schemings, the paltry

jealousies, the social littlenesses and rivalries around her were matters of which Lady Peyton was absolutely unconscious.

Such knowledge, in the very nature of things, could not come near her. True, her own name was freely canvassed, and she was deeply concerned in the present agitation, though she knew it not.

"Would the service never end!" thought Miss Medlicott, in her impatience girding even against the melody of the "sacred flute," and finding the long concluding hymn a weariness to the flesh. "What, oh! what had dear Mr. Westerton to say?" Could it be (oh! Sleeksby!) that a tender feeling towards herself was about to find vent in words? But no; the agitation that was evident to the close observer in the reverend gentleman's demeanour partook more of perturbation than happy flutterings of spirit. Besides, had she not given him every possible chance only the Friday evening before, giving Mrs. Mandeville the slip by the post-office, and coasting round Mrs. Barnstable-Ambler—as a mariner cir-

cumvents a sunken rock—just at the turn by
the mill?

Did she not know that the "dear Thing"
("thing" with a capital T), as the ladies
called the curate among themselves, would be
coming across the fields from a small mission
church in an outlying hamlet, that was occasionally edified by a Friday-evening service?
Were not her calculations correct to a nicety?
Was not Mr. Westerton most kind—though,
alas! no more than kind? Did she not en-
large, after she had got over the first surprise
of seeing him, upon the inestimable benefit
to be derived from having a reliable and
trusted guide always at hand? Had not
Mrs. Mandeville heard of the encounter, and
reproached her friend for a slight indiscretion
in walking thus alone with so seductive an
individual, and, it might be, "giving cause
for tongues"?

"A married woman can do a great deal
that in a—girl" (the little hesitation over the
word "girl" was delicious, hitting delicately
at Miss Medlicott's seven-and-twenty summers)

—" er—in a girl is apt to have an air of imprudence," said Mrs. Mandeville lowering her undoubtedly handsome eyes, as if some unseemly sight were presented to their chaste gaze.

" Yes, dear," said Miss Medlicott, thinking what fun she would have with Mrs. Ambler presently over this gracious advice.

"I only speak for your own good," continued Mrs. Mandeville suavely.

Valerie Medlicott's black eyes flashed dangerously for a moment. But she kept her head, and replied with equal politeness—

" Yes, dear."

Emboldened by this meekness on the part of her victim, the other again took up her parable.

"I do not doubt that Mr. Westerton must have thought you a little—venturesome, to say the least."

" He did not seem to mind, dear."

" He is so considerate for others. He would not show it."

" Anyway, he is never blunt and rude

in his way of speaking . . . . like Mr. Ulla-thorne."

This was a home-thrust, and pierced the joints of the opponent's armour; for it was well known that Mrs. Mandeville had suffered grievous repulse at the hands of the Rev. Mr. Ullathorne—a fact which yielded that lady's friends much secret delight.

However, all these things happened in the past, and our story ought to be harking forward; so we will return to Scarsdale Church, where the congregation is pouring out, flowing down the steep steps like an avalanche, and then spreading this way and that, and so thinning into a fringe of scattered figures, the more distant ones but dimly seen in the autumn evening haze.

Mr. Westerton was out of his surplice and had slipped by the Rector like an eel before you could have said "Jack Robinson," or even "Jack," for the matter of that. He had an uncomfortable feeling that the eye of Maister Straw was on him, and indeed, lest there should be any doubt on the subject, that functionary gave a hollow and sepulchral cough as the curate's coat-tails disappeared round the corner of the vestry-door.

Mr. Westerton was always better than his actions, and the sound of that cough haunted him as the memory of a reproach might have done. He was the sport of his own egregious vanity, and he knew it; also he knew that he was on the way to do a mean and ignoble action, yet could not resist the temptation of the prestige that was sure to follow. Hardly had he passed the stile leading into the fields that sloped down gently towards the Meadows, when he caught sight of two figures on ahead, linked indeed all lovingly, yet fired with most unholy jealousy notwithstanding. The spidery figure of Miss Medlicott and the more substantial one of Mrs. Mandeville moved steadily onwards. Not a glance backward betrayed a knowledge of the "dear Thing's" propinquity, not a prick of the ears betrayed a consciousness of the hurrying step behind. They were *so* surprised when Mr. Westerton overtook them!

"The church was quite close this afternoon, was it not?" said Mrs. Mandeville taking, as indeed became her, being a married woman, the initiative. Valerie hung back, bashful-like, and gave bright, inquiring glances at the curate from the shelter of her friend's arm.

"Yes," said Mr. Westerton, "it was warm, and I really thought a stroll before my usual Sunday-evening's theological studies——"

"Really, dear Mr. Westerton, you work too hard, you do indeed," cooed Mrs. Mandeville; "you should allow yourself more relaxation. We also came for a stroll; Valerie complained of headache."

Mr. Westerton murmured his sympathy; but they were all beating about the bush, and they knew it.

There was "metal more attractive" hidden away, yet making itself felt.

Both ladies were indeed convinced that Mr. Westerton had "something to say," though upon the probable subject of the precious communication they were in a haze of un-

certainty.   Their minds were also disturbed
as to what had become of Mrs. Barnstable
Ambler.   They both felt that at all times
she was anything but straight in her tactics,
and deep distrust of a common enemy was a
mutual bond.   In their sentimental relations
with Mr. Westerton, Mrs. Mandeville was
weighted with a ponderous husband—stout,
florid, loud-voiced, a hindrance in every way.
Valerie was hampered by a shrewd mother
and a train of objectionable schoolboy brothers.
Mrs. Ambler alone was free, owned a charming little house down below the fall of the hill
from Upper Scarsdale, and from her position
as a widow could entertain her friends as she
pleased, without "fear of tongues."

This was very well indeed, as she kept a
good cook and a neat waiting-maid, and was
the first person to introduce into Scarsdale
a custom faintly foreshadowing the now universal five-o'clock-tea.

"She's forty if she's a day," said Valerie in
a moment of exasperation to Mrs. Mandeville.

"A woman with a figure like that may be

any age, it doesn't matter a fig," replied the other; "though how any one can see any attraction in a woman with a nose like a beak——"

Silence alone could express the indignation of the pair at this stage of affairs. Mrs. Mandeville called Miss Medlicott "Valerie," and Miss Medlicott called Mrs. Mandeville "Charlotte"—even once going so far as "Lottie"—for several weeks after this mutual outburst; but, alas! disputations arose, and retreat was the order of the day. These shadows, however, again passed, and, as we have seen, the two wandered arm-in-arm among the fields and trees, and were so found, like a brace of Siamese twins, by the Reverend Sleeksby Westerton on that grey November evening. Every now and again one or the other cast a furtive glance to this side or to that, but not a sign of the sweeping lines of Mrs. Ambler's black silk skirts or dainty bonnet of grey ostrich tips was to be seen.

"We live in strange times here," said Mr.

Westerton at last, with a significant shake of
the head. "What with young Peyton's sudden
departure, the disappearance of the groom and
the boy Spool, the madness of that terrible
old woman, Mother Bond, whose case really
ought to be laid before the magistrates, and
—I must add—a certain more pronounced reserve and hauteur towards myself on the part
of——"

"Oh, do not!" cried Miss Medlicott, in the
tone of one who is conscious of a sudden
twinge of toothache; "it is *too* painful a subject. Dear Mr. Westerton, may we not safely
take the view that these trials are sent for the
discipline of the just?"

Mr. Westerton, with his big eyes cast down,
his mouth agape in a silly smile, and his hands
folded finger to finger, was doubtless supposed
to represent the just; but he did not look
the character well. The fact was he had been
making himself very busy about affairs at the
Hall, and the Rector and Alison had shown
every disposition to what he called "quelch"
him. His only acquaintance with the Peytons

was an occasional dinner at their table—times when he was excruciatingly ill at ease, but to which he looked forward with rapture, and back upon with exultation; consequently any attempts upon his part to discuss the affairs of the family with the Rector or Alison were ruthlessly nipped in the bud. It was on such occasions that Mr. Darling had most cause to remind himself forcibly of old college days and his old chum Stanley Westerton.

The question of the discipline of the just having been settled to every one's satisfaction, Mr. Westerton looked important, also a little ashamed, coughed, hesitated, and finally made known the fact that he had had "rather a strange experience" the previous evening. He had been walking down by the Falls, a very considerable distance, as they all knew, from Scarsdale Upper or Scarsdale Lower. His thoughts had been somewhat intently fixed on certain matters (here each lady was conscious of a sort of tremble in the other's arm, and, as though by mutual consent, took up an independent position), when all at once he was brought, as it were, at once to earth (this term delicately hinted at thoughts that communed with the skies, and did not prove as interesting to his hearers as the more possible mundane explanation of the previous sentence), by meeting at a sudden turn—Mr. Lance Peyton and Miss Alison Darling.

The ladies were at once puzzled and excited. It was no wonderful thing that old companions and close friends should take a walk down by the Falls—why then was the superior mind of Sleeksby Westerton impressed by the circumstance?

For this simple reason: the Rector's daughter had her head turned away from her companion, and the tears were streaming down her face. Lance was pale, deeply troubled, and so absorbed in whatever he was saying that he appeared to be unconscious of the curate's existence; indeed, brushed by him in the rudest possible manner. Miss Alison, though, saw him, in spite of her sad, drowned eyes, and acknowledged his hasty salute. Then the pair passed on round the turn of the pathway, and Mr. Westerton was left alone to meditate upon what he had seen.

"Sly thing!" said Mrs. Mandeville when the interesting recital was finished.

"How shocking!" said Valerie, "making such a display of her feelings, you know."

"Well, I don't know," said Mr. Westerton, feebly protesting. "I hardly think shocking is quite the word, really now. The affair was startling, I allow. It shows that an undercurrent has been going on."

"Of which we have known nothing!" put in Mrs. Mandeville with asperity. "I have always thought Alison Darling *much* overrated by many, but I hardly imagined her to be designing."

"She is playing for high stakes—to be the lady of the Old Hall. If Sir Marmaduke only knew!" said Miss Medlicott.

"If so," said Mr. Westerton, "she has been playing a losing game; for she looked a great deal more like blighted hopes than anything else. They might have been taking an everlasting farewell, don't you know?"

"If Alison Darling only knew the delusive nature of such hopes, how they turn to dust and ashes in the mouth," said Mrs. Mandeville, with a meaning glance at the tall, black-coated gentleman by her side, "she would give them up without a sigh."

This alluded to certain confidences the lady had made to her spiritual adviser and friend as to the "desolation of heart" of which she was at times conscious; confidences that at one time Mr. Westerton had received with avidity, as tending indirectly to pet and coddle his overweening vanity, but which by this time had begun to pall upon him considerably. The *femme incomprise* was, indeed, Mrs. Mandeville's favourite *rôle*, and she had tried the matrimonial confidence trick upon the late curate, Mr. Ullathorne; but that gentleman mistook the purport of her murmured plaints, taking it that she was touching upon Mr. Mandeville's tendency to rheumatic gout.

True, he gave her his most cordial sympathy on the supposed grievance, and offered to go and play a game of chess with the sufferer now and then, and " cheer him up, don't you know." But was such commonplace density food for the hunger of the heart ?

In Mr. Ullathorne Mrs. Mandeville fondly fancied she had met the man destined to be that " friend of her soul" for whom she longed. She was mistaken ; but kind Fate had removed him, and the gentle-hearted Sleeksby reigned in his stead. Surely even he was not going to fail her !

Of late she had sometimes had misgivings. Mr. Westerton did not return his friend's confidential glance. He chose to ignore the tender relations of the past—the little notes sent to his lodgings by a trusty hand, the pages of a certain " diary of a soul," lent to him under the most solemn vows of eternal silence. Valerie, too, on her part, fancied the spiritual friend, whom she had hoped would develop into an earthly lover, *distrait* in manner now and then. Medlicott the lawyer was a man of means ; he had come into a good share of county practice, and dined out a good deal (without his family) among the county folks. Scarsdale was of opinion that the curate might do worse; for who would be ill-natured enough to tell him that Valerie had thrown herself at the head of "the Rev. Ullathorne," and sung songs to the accompaniment of a banjo to his predecessor, an amiable musical maniac, who tried to start a choral service, and had aspirations in the direction of a surpliced choir?

People said it would really be a good thing for Valerie Medlicott to be settled in life at last.

" Of course," said Mr. Westerton, glancing keenly first at one of his companions and then at the other, " this little matter remains sacredly between us three."

" Certainly, certainly; sacredly between us three," said Mrs. Mandeville.

She put a nasty little emphasis upon the word " three " that made Mr. Westerton flush up to the roots of his pale-coloured hair; but the " shades of night were falling fast,"

and mercifully veiled the reverend gentleman's blushes.

Finally the friends parted, Mrs. Mandeville
insisting upon Miss Medlicott going home
to tea with her, thereby ensuring that no
undesirable *tête-à-tête* should take place, and
also engaging Mr. Westerton to dinner at
The Beeches, her suburban abode, for the
following evening, gracefully including Valerie
in the invitation.

Then the ladies departed, their figures
growing gradually more and more indistinct
in the grey and silvery gloom; for the nights
were still frosty, and a chill mist crept along
over the grass.

Mr. Westerton betook himself homewards,
contemplating in his mind's eye as he did so
the refreshment which he knew his landlady
would have all ready prepared for him—the
tea, that had been standing till it was black
in colour and vapid in taste; the toast,
leathery and unsatisfying; the salt butter,
" washed " to imitate fresh as nearly as might
be; and then another picture arose—one

which called up a smile and a smirk, and
made the curate's fingers steal up to the
side-locks of his hair and give them a tender
pat ; made him stand a moment, give a hasty
glance round as though he feared his two
female devotees might reappear at some unexpected corner, and then——

No, it would be too bad to say that the
reverend gentleman made a bolt of it ; but
his mode of progression might have given
colour to such a vulgarism, and it is certain
that he was slightly breathless as he rang
at a certain garden-door in an ivy-covered
wall.

Maister Straw, chancing to pass the corner
of the narrow road that led to this secluded
abode, caught sight of the waiting figure,
saw the door open, saw the ivy-covered wall
absorb Mr. Westerton ; slapped his thigh
with a sounding slap, and ejaculated to the
gathering shades—

"Dang the lot of 'em, and ten to one on
the widow !"

Could he have seen Mr. Westerton—his

feet, at Mrs. Barnstable Ambler's earnest entreaty, comfortably posed on the fender, his teacup in one hand, a piece of hot Sally Lunn, crisp and juicy, in the other, and a fatuous smile on his face as he gazed at the goddess who presided at the cosy round table, with its shaded lamp and ample supply of delicate viands—surely he would have doubled, or even trebled, his bet on the issue of events.

As to Mrs. Mandeville and Miss Medlicott (also taking their tea over a cosy fire, and discussing the possibilities and impossibilities of Alison's troubles), words would fail me to describe what would have been their indignation could they have known what a viper they had (of course metaphorically, and with the very strictest propriety) warmed in their bosoms.

"Valerie," said Mrs. Mandeville (they were at the Christian-name stage just now), "that little child—an orphan niece, is it not?—of the landlady's at dear Mr. Westerton's lodgings is, I believe, ill. I think I shall go and

see if I can be of any use. Of course I feel
the delicacy of the situation, a bachelor's
lodgings and all that, but I am anxious about
our friend. I think he burns the midnight
oil; perhaps with fevered brow studies far
on into the night. I may glean something.
The position would be compromising for you;
but there are many things a married woman
can do."

"I am never in any danger of forgetting
that, Charlotte," replied Miss Valerie, not
without asperity, and raising her voice a little
too high, for Aaron Mandeville, Esq., or "Old
Mandeville," as Scarsdale generally called him,
was asleep in the next room with a bandana
over his face, and it was of consequence that
he should not be roughly aroused from his
Sabbath slumbers, or he was apt to be what
his wife called "tetchy," having even been
known to speak of Miss Medlicott as "spider-
legs," and ask of a listening world why she
was always having tea in his parlour.

After a silence, during which the gentle
vibration of a snore assured the ladies that

all was safe, Valerie, with some hesitation, made a suggestion.

"I don't see why I shouldn't go with you, dear."

"With me!" said the other, with a sudden upward curl of the lip and quick stare—signs only too familiar to her friend.

"Yes; I should so like to see the room where *he* writes and dreams"—"perhaps of me," she added to her own heart.

"Valerie," said Mrs. Mandeville, making mouths over her words, as she always did when angry, and holding her head at quite a painful angle, "there is sometimes a want of refinement about things you say that grates upon me—ger-rates upon me, Valerie."

Let us draw a veil over the rest, and content ourselves with expressing a pious hope that Old Mandeville slept through it. Meanwhile the ungrateful object of all this tender contention had his feet tucked up on Mrs. Barnstable Ambler's fender, and was confiding to that lady (forgetful, alas! of the "council of three" and the vow of silence)

his adventures anent the Rector's daughter
and the Squire's son.

And Alison Darling was "dreeing her weird."
A very bitter, cruel weird, borne with noble
courage and womanly endurance.

At first, after Lance returned from that
dreary ceremony, seeing his brother off to
India, he seemed more and more drawn
towards the charmed circle at the Rectory.
In that atmosphere of home-love, sympathy,
and truest union, he doubtless found some
balm for sorrows that had come upon him
unexpectedly, and could not be told.

Neither Alison nor her father knew of
those interviews in the dark oak library,
carried on far into the night; but they read
the signs of a trouble unknown to them in
the dark passionate face of Sir Marmaduke's
son. Always wilful and ready to be un-
reasonable, Lance now became morbid and
gloomy, morose in manner even to the good
Rector, silent and brooding, even when by
Alison's side.

Nothing calls forth the full force of the tenderness and passion that a true woman gives to the man she loves, like the sight of that man in sorrow and sadness. Day by day, in these troublous times, the girl grew to feel more and more that her life was bound up in that of another; that trial and grief for herself would be light burdens indeed compared to that of seeing that dear head bowed, those dear eyes clouded by gloom. In her dreams she saw him with his face hidden in his arms, his hands clenched in abject abandonment, and yet was held back by some irresistible power, against which it was vain to struggle, from clasping her arms about him and lifting the shrouded face with her tender, loving hands. The love that is true shines brightest in the dark; hitherto the maiden heart had slumbered, conscious indeed of a silver thread running through the strand, of life a melody thrilling through the gamut of the days, but hardly realising herself as a woman whose heart had wholly escaped from her own keeping.

Now the awakening had come.

The passionate longing to help and comfort,
the restlessness in his absence, the bounding
of her pulses at the sound of his footstep, the
never-ceasing undercurrent of her thoughts
that set towards him as a river towards the
sea, the prayers that rose from heart to lips
on his behalf as she knelt in the sacred
quietude of her own chamber—all these signs,
and many another besides, told her that Love
had arisen in his might, and " smote the
chords of life " to a trembling ecstasy of
melody covering a thrill of pain.   What was
this dark shadow for ever brooding over the
man she loved ?

True, he must miss the bright and genial
" boy "—the " boy of boys," as the Rector
once called Cyril in an outburst of loving
delight.   But even that would not account
for all ; and strange rumours were afloat—
little nasty innuendoes that stung and irri-
tated you like gnats ; things hard to catch
and hold, yet making you conscious of their
unwelcome presence.   The morbid fanaticism

that was known to dominate the Squire of
the Old Hall was said to be deepening and
intensifying. There were whispers of nights
when his bed had never been what the
housemaids called "slep' in;" of lights seen
by chance passers-by at strange, unholy
hours, glimmering through the belt of trees
that hedged the old house round; of hushed,
yet hotly disputing voices heard in the
night-time; of my Lady seated "like a
statute," as Mrs. Dutton had it, with Hound's
great head on her knees, and his wistful
eyes looking pleadingly up into her face.
He must have wondered, poor faithful soul!
what had come of the sunshine of the house,
why all went so sadly, and why the step
he was ever listening for never resounded in
the corridors!

One morning a strange thing happened.
Lady Peyton was in the room that had been
Cyril's, like an uneasy spirit revisiting the
scene of past joys. She often lingered in
that silent and deserted chamber, often took
"the boy's" letters there to read, for news

had come across the sea, and she knew that
her darling was safe so far.   Such letters,
too—bright and hopeful, as though the pen
that wrote them had been dipped in sunshine,
tender, loving—oh! such precious things to
the eyes that read them, often through a
mist of happy tears!   On this occasion she
had just folded the flimsy sheet, when the
door was pushed firmly open, and in stalked
Hound, a bit of something white sticking
out of his muzzle.   Now the dog had a bad
habit of picking up pieces of paper and
carrying them about, and had been corrected
for it more than once, so his mistress chid
him, and took hold of the edge of the paper;
but he clenched his teeth, lifted his upper lip,
and showed signs of temper, then suddenly repented, and dropped the fragment at her feet.

It was an envelope, burnt across, yet not
wholly destroyed, enough being left to show
that it had been directed to Launcelot Peyton,
and that the date of the post-mark was the
day before, while the sheet in Lady Peyton's
hand bore that of a fortnight back.

"How strange," thought Lady Peyton, "that Lance should never tell me he had heard from his brother!"

Hound swung his tail from side to side, proud to find his small offering taken so much notice of. But my Lady's face grew pale and drawn, and she had no smile for her favourite. Stay! a bit of notepaper is in the torn envelope. She draws it out and spreads it open. Part of it is charred and black, but she can decipher the words: "Alison—sister—" and then a fragment of a lower line, "I long to hear——"

It is closing in dusk by now, but she is used to going out at all times and seasons, and her tall stately figure, followed by Hound, soon passes along under the limes and copper-beeches; she has passed the lodge, and is on her way to the village. A long trudge, some might say, but Marion Lady Peyton is none of your listless fine ladies. She has a grand swinging walk, and soon gains the fall of the road towards the church. How beautiful it looks, with the moon just rising through a grey mist beyond it, and its tall spire showing dark and taper against the sky !

But she does not linger; she passes on, turns down sharply, and in another moment is asking for stamps at the post-office, an institution that makes itself generally useful as a chandler's and sweetstuff shop as well.

The official is all attention. My Lady is, as always, courteous, remarking upon the beauty of the afternoon, and the early moon rise.

"This is the Indian mail day ?" she says, with a little pathetic smile.

The answer comes promptly, even eagerly—

"Yes, my lady. We were glad to see there was a letter from Mr. Cyril for his brother."

She said good-night, her voice even and sweet, her kindly look showing that she took no offence at the betrayed interest in her family affairs. In a little town such as Scarsdale every one's affairs were public property.

So that was it, was it ?

The post-bag was taken to Sir Marmaduke's study every morning, and he alone had the key. He kept abnormally early hours at times—had, she knew, been up at six that very day. He had come into breakfast with the letters in his hand. She had not dared to show impatience, but her heart throbbed; she stretched out her hand.

"It is Indian mail day," she said, with a thrill in her voice that made Lance look up at her quickly.

For all answer Sir Marmaduke laid down and spread out the letters.

It was a silent lie!

Loving words had been stifled, both brothers defrauded. A voice from across the sea had been strangled into silence. It was a lie, though no word was uttered.

What could she do?

Could a wife go to her son and tell him that his father was dishonoured? And why had the cruel theft been committed?

What motive had been strong enough to drive Sir Marmaduke to such extremity?

Lady Peyton was as one groping in the dark ; she stumbled and blundered, having none to guide her.

It was but a few days later that the Rev. Sleeksby Westerton met Alison Darling with the Squire's son — met her with her sweet face bathed in tears, and her fair cheek pale and wan.

CHAPTER VII.

"GOOD-BYE, SWEETHEART, GOOD-BYE."

ALISON and Lance stood in the rose-garden. The day was one of those, strangely soft and warm for the time of year, that sometimes come to us as the forerunners of the spring awakening; messengers on ahead to cheer us with the fair promise of May.

The rose-wreaths, brown and leafless, yet showed pinky-green buds here and there; a thrush—earliest first-comer of the year's choristers—piped on a tree hard by, and the pigeons cooed upon the gables. Yet these sights and sounds of hope found no echo in the hearts of the two who stood side by side, and hand in hand.

They had returned from a walk down to the Falls. They had listened to the rushing of the waters as to the beating of their own

hearts, sounds assuredly as full and tumul-
tuous. There had been no intention of each
betraying to the other the secret that had
grown with the years; but Lance had looked
pale and haggard, and his eyes were heavy;
now and again he would press his hand to his
brow; and the sweet face turned upon him,
full of such tender, womanly sympathy and
pity, had overset his resolution.

There had not been many words. Just
"Alison, my dearest!" and a soft reply,
"Lance, dear Lance!" Then a moment or
two that the woman would never forget,
when her lover's lips touched hers, and his
heart beat fast against her own; a moment
in which the trees, almost meeting above her
head, seemed as the arches of some grand
cathedral, and the rush and rhythm of the
waters as the chanting of a song of marriage joy.

After that—what?

The blackness of desolation, a man's half-
frenzied self-reproaches, a man's bitter distress—so bitter that at last all thought of

her own bewilderment died out, and Alison turned comforter.

Incoherent, strange to her ears, were the utterances of the man she loved. He had looked haggard and worn; she had turned upon him her lovely face full of gentlest sympathy and pity; a little quiver about the corners of the tender mouth, a dewy brightness shining in the azure eyes, and, in a moment, hot words of passion had burst from his lips—the friend and playfellow had become the lover.

As in a trance of joy the girl listened to the sweetest music that had ever yet fallen on her ears; and then, like the crash and the jar of discord, came the knowledge that some barrier lay between them, that fruition could never follow promise, that their joy must be turned into bitterness, that for them the sun of hope must set in the darkness of night. The good and pure are unselfish; the unselfish are ever brave. Tears might fall down Alison's sweet face, her cheek grow pale as lilies' petals, but she was not one to whine.

A supreme effort was called for, and the call upon her resolution was not met by failure. She seemed lifted above this world, separated from all else save the man who told her one moment that he loved her, passionately, intensely, fondly, and, in the next, that nothing lay before them save an eternal farewell. That in this fateful ramble they met and passed the Rev. Sleeksby Westerton made little impression upon Alison. She was at all times one who rather shunned those she disliked, as dreading the unpleasantness of repulsion, and the tall, somewhat shifty-eyed curate made small impression upon her inner consciousness, and she gave little thought to the mere accidents of life, in which light the encounter with Mr. Westerton presented itself to her.

Her whole soul was up in arms to meet the emergency of feeling that had come upon her. The cup she had longed for was but placed at her lips when a cruel hand dashed it aside—why she knew not.

She was suffering horribly, but she must

not yet make her moan. There could be no sin or wrong in the love Lance bore her, or in the tenderness that welled up in her heart towards him like a fount of living water. What, then, meant these self-reproaches, these lamentations, that were almost like curses on his lips?

"I have been a brute, a villain, to let my tongue get the better of my head. Alison, forgive me!" he said, crushing the hand he held till the rings she wore ran into the tender flesh.

The girl was no sentimental fool, but a true, passionate-hearted woman, ready to speak up in her own cause; ready to suffer, if needs be, but resolved to know where the bitter necessity lay.

"Was it not rather your heart that spoke?" she said, looking at him piteously with her drowned eyes. "Do you not love me, Lance—O Lance!"

Did he not love her?

His haggard, yearning eyes, the pale trouble of his face, answered her, and yet——

"We can be nothing to each other—nothing," he said, setting his teeth hard to bite back a sob. "When people love, it must be all or nothing, and fate has decreed that with us it must be nothing. Alison, I am going away. I meant to ask you to bid me——" Then, with a muttered oath, "No, no; not 'God speed,' but only to say with those dear lips, 'Lance, old friend, dear playmate of the bygone happy years, I forgive you.'"

They stood in the rose-garden, by the rose-brier that now held no store of scented leaves, but whose tiny buds were growing under the impulse born of coming warmth and joy. Less happy were the budding hopes of the pure woman-heart, fated to know no sweet summertide of joy.

Yet out of pain grew exaltation and the noble magnificence of a perfect and passionate love. On Alison's face shone the light of resolve.

"If, though you cannot tell me why, it needs be that we must really part, then,

Lance, dear Lance, I do forgive you. I do not grudge you anything that I have given to you. I have always thought that love was not love indeed that could grudge what it gave, and I shall always know that you did love me—always, always, always. It will be sweet to remember that."

He had sunk upon the wide, low seat in the alcove; his face was hidden in his hands. The sunshine fell full upon him; a thrush lilted in the copper-beech hard by; and a little blue tit ran madly up the bark of a larch tree, crying, " Chir-a-ra-ra-ree !" as if in fancy he was climbing to his little nest to be.

What mockery these sights and sounds of coming joy. He heard the song of the thrush, as we all hear and note small sounds in moments of deep pain, and hated the bird for singing; he heard the merry cry of the tit; he felt the bright, unwonted sunshine, the *avant courier* of the summer that was coming ; but above all these, and dominating all, was the picture of that face, brave and beautiful, full of such passionate, sweet tenderness, such

womanly strength, such noble courage—from
this he had had to cower away as from a sight
he could not bear to look upon.

"Lance, dear Lance, I do forgive you.
You have stolen nothing. I gave it all to you
freely—freely! You know, dear, you have
always been a naughty, wilful boy, have you
not? Strange and wayward in your ways,
full of fancies, sometimes brooding and given
to odd moods. Well, I want you always to
remember that I loved you—like that—that
even your faults were dear to me — that I
should never have murmured, never chidden
you. You see, as these things will never be,
I have to blow my own trumpet a little; cry
myself up, and tell you—try to make you
see——"

"Do not tell me—I know. Do not try to
make me see," he cried, starting to his feet.
"I see already the glimpse of the heaven I
shall never reach. Alison, your gentle words
cannot comfort me. I feel—I must ever feel
—that I have defrauded you, stolen your dear
heart on false pretences; but, believe me, I

did not mean it so.   I did not know; I
believed that I was free."

She looked up at him with a little pucker
between her brows, but she would not probe
him with questions, as a meaner woman
would have done.   She had made her quiet
appeal, and that appeal had failed.   She
would now be steadfast and endure.   Besides,
he was in trouble; sorely put to it, she knew
not how or why; and she must comfort him,
console him, sustain him; it was her woman's
privilege.

"You will meet many better men, many
who will love you," he broke out at last.

"Many better men, perhaps," she echoed
wearily, "but none dearer."

A wild light shone up into his eyes.

"Alison, I will not give up all hope.   I
see one glimmer yet—a desperate hope, perhaps, but still a hope.   Do not lose heart, my
darling."

But Alison did not believe in the glimmer.
She saw too well some dire and cruel necessity
was binding the will of the man before her,

as his limbs might have been bound with cords. She read despair in the depths of his dark, deep-set eyes; she knew in her heart of hearts that their steps must be on either side of the river—the cold, deep, rushing river of time—not hand in hand upon its flower-pied bank. She might strain her eyes to catch a glimpse of his figure moving on; but never should they wander side by side, quarrelling and making it up again, pouting, laughing, merry and sad by turns, as in the dear old days. When they were children Lance would scold her; he slapped her once, and she, being a bit of a virago in her way, slapped him back; but just let any one else be pert to the Rector's little daughter, and woe betide them if Launcelot, her knight, were near!

Well, well, she was tamed since those days. He had hit her a cruel blow now; but she had no longing to hit him back.

Once more he sat on the old garden-seat under the pent-house of the archway in the rosery, his face hidden in his hands, Alison bending over him like some fair image of heavenliest pity. Herself was all forgotten. She hardly remembered her own pain ; only to comfort him, only to be strong for his sake, that was what she strove after. At last she laid her hand lovingly on the dark bowed head, stroking ever so gently the hair that was smooth and shining as the raven's wing. Something of benediction—of valediction too —was in that touch, and under its spell the strong man quivered ; more than that, he let his head fall against that gentle bosom, and Alison, clasping him, broke into bitter sobs and sighing.

Then he rose and caught her, crushing her to him close and fast, while his lips pressed hers in mad, despairing kisses, and she felt his hot tears falling on her face.

After that, in a moment as it seemed, Alison was alone in the rose-garden, with the budding branches gently swaying round her, and the thrush finishing his evening-song.

How still she sat, her hands folded in her lap, her head resting back against the old grey stone wall !

A little frog in a sleek, bright-spotted skin hopped out of the rose-bushes and looked at her with his golden eyes; a robin perched so close to her that she might have touched him with her hand; the cheeky little tit swung himself upside down on the spray of climbing rose just above her head.

She was so still, so still, that sleeping princess in their midst! Perhaps they thought that she was dead, and robin was about to take her measure for a shroud of ivy and laurel leaves, the only foliage at hand.

Alison was striving to fight the battle of pain all alone.

There were loving eyes to be cheated, loving hearts whose peace must be guarded as a mother guards a sleeping child.

The household tradition that "mamma's room" must never be invaded by anxiety or sorrow, if tender care and watching could keep such unwelcome guests away, had grown with Alison's growth, and strengthened with her strength. Even now the burning tears must be kept back lest her eyes should grow

too red-rimmed for concealment to be possible.
Floating over the deep current of her own
suffering, like a bird's plaintive cry over a
storm-tossed sea, was the thought, "Mamma,
mamma—what can I do to spare her in this
sorrow that has come upon her child?"

Presently greater strength came with striving. Alison rose slowly and, with effort;
then her step grew firmer. As she passed
the window of her mother's room, Mrs.
Darling was visible in her reclining chair,
and, catching sight of her daughter, waved
her hand.

Where do women gather their strength
from at such moments? They are cleverer
at this chicanery than men are.

Alison returned the greeting. The dear
eyes at the window were dim with patient
years of pain; they could not see the pallid
cheek, the heavy tear-dimmed eye.

Then there was the open door to pass.

Alison hummed a tune, a line from an old-
fashioned song her mother loved.

"How happy the child is!" said Mrs.

Darling to herself, letting her hand lift and fall to the rhythm; "and to think that I was once as light-hearted!"

A tear gathered, and she wiped it away. She had many things to be thankful for— many beautiful things in her life, many precious treasures of joy in her home—but, like a caged bird, she sometimes longed for liberty and movement.

Meanwhile, above, Alison had gained her own little room. It seemed to her like some quiet sanctuary in which a hunted fugitive might seek rest and shelter. How brightly the sunlight shimmered into the room, making a pattern of trembling leaf-shadows on the floor!

There on the window-sill lay the open book she had discarded but a few hours ago. What were the last words she had read?

"Lord! we know what we are, but know not what we may be."

Ah! poor Ophelia! she too was cruelly bereft; she too could say, "And I of ladies most deject and wretched!"

"Most deject and wretched!" How the words seemed to ring in Alison's ears, to put out the shining of the sun, to silence the lilting of the birds amid the ivy, the birds who were waking to the hope and promise of summer; while she—while she—— Still she would not weep, but her breast rose and fell, her breath came thickly, she pressed her hand over her burning eyes, and soon she lay all along, face downwards, on her snow-white bed, and there was silence in that pretty chamber.

There is a simple teaching of which the initial words run this: "Our Father, which art in heaven." He is not a hard avenging Deity, somewhere very far off, delighting in suffering, craving for vicarious pain, but a loving, tender Father, One who feels for His children, even as the earthly father for the cherished little ones about his knee. . . .

This teaching had been Alison's; this light had lightened the home of her childhood, guided the heart of her youth.

It did not fail her now.

"Save me, O God, for the waters are come in unto my soul!" Then, above the storm and the tempest of pain, the still, small voice of faith and resignation : "Nevertheless, be it unto me according to Thy will."

Never had Alison been sweeter, brighter, more tender to her mother, more ready with her sympathy, than through the rest of that long evening. She even deceived her father's eyes, and this says much for her histrionic powers, for the Rector's eyes were keen as well as kind, or, as Maister Straw put it, "he could see through a stone wall same as a pane o' glass, an' when ither folk had to fetch t' ladder and speer over top on 't."

The next day was Sunday, with its many calls and manifold duties.

All went just as usual, save that Lance did not show at church, and the dear, good Rector thought that he had never within his remembrance heard his daughter play so well or with so much feeling and pathos. He was quite uplifted in spirit by the sound of her clear, sweet voice leading the rest :—

"Though Thou should'st call me to resign
What most I prize—it ne'er was mine—
I only yield Thee what is Thine.
Thy will be done."

The very spirit of renunciation seemed em-
bodied in the thrill that permeated her voice,
in the music of the organ as called forth by
her deft fingers.

"My dear," he said complacently, as the
two walked home together after afternoon
service, " I never heard you sing and play
better than you did to-day. Really the
rendering of that voluntary, ' It is decreed,'
was fine, fine, decidedly fine. I must not
flatter my girl, but I am proud of her. I
really——"

He beamed all over his kindly face ; he
hummed a stave of the air that had been
played as a voluntary ; he was in great spirits,
was the Rector.

"I am glad I pleased you so much to-day,
papa," said Alison simply.

Something in the tone of her voice made
him turn and look at her keenly.

"You are pale, child," he said. " You have

been taking it out of yourself too much. You must rest, my dear; I really must insist upon it. It does not do to be too exacting even with energy and strength like yours. No, no; not at all, not at all."

Alison was silent.

What a strange experience was the girl passing through!

All around her and about her so familiar: the dear old home coming into sight, with here and there a light twinkling through the trees: when she turned to look back, the church, supreme, enthroned, beautiful against the mellow sky of the dying day, with slender spire reaching out towards the stars, and the village houses clustering about the feet of the sanctuary like children about the mother's knee. The dogs were waiting in a cluster at the Rectory-gate, because they knew it was Sunday, and dare not come a step farther, but making the most of the situation by violent agitation of tails, and now and again a yelp of impatience—all these things the same, and yet not the same, because looked upon " with a difference," looked upon through eyes dim with a passion of regret, aching with a sense of longing.

Was it a day, a year, or an age since she last saw the dark, agonised face of the man she loved ? Was it only yesterday that she listened to his pleadings for pardon, his bitter self-reproaches ; or was it in a time very far off—in a dream, perhaps ? How was it that a silence seemed to be everywhere, since she could hear that voice no more ? Had it filled all the world—all the world of a woman's heart, and now, now, was there " no sound of violins," no music in earth or heaven for her strained ear ?

Lance had spoken of a hope, yet, even in so speaking, his voice had held a ring of hopelessness.

Was there, could there be, a chance that this barrier between them should give way ? It was wonderful how little she dwelt upon the nature of the barrier. Lance said that something stood between them ; he suffered in this severance as well as she. Was it some

wrong thing, some past sin of his that hung
about him like a chain?

What if it were? She should not love
him less because he had been wrong. If
he had sinned, and was reaping a bittter
harvest, why, then he needed her all the
more—all the more. It was little she could
give him, since he had decreed that they
should part; but he would have the memory
of her tenderness, her sympathy; the touch
of her hand on his sad, bowed head, of her
lips meeting his.

She had no notion of giving with a niggard
hand, for the short and precious moments
when it was in her power to show him all
her heart.

Why should she, since she loved him?

It seemed they must go each on their
several ways; but he should be able to look
back and say to his own heart, "She loved
me, she loved me, she loved me."

It was a poor kind of comfort, perhaps, but
it was all she had to give him. She did not
believe in the love that doles itself out grain

by grain, and stops to give until quite sure that a full return is to be got; that just so much is deserved and no more—not she!

To give with both hands and with all her heart, even as she had done (not knowing) all through the long years, that was Alison's idea of loving.

That it had brought with it an intolerable pain—a suffering so keen that under it her young life seemed ready to faint and fail—all this she counted as nothing. It was not too great a price to pay, if Lance should be the gainer; if some sweet store of tender memories should be his to help him on his way.

The God in whom she trusted would not fail her. If this joy must be denied her, if this fair plant of love must bear neither blossom nor fruit, then her feet were destined to follow in some other pathway; there was other work in the world for her to do.

It was hard to have to wait the solution of the riddle of her life. Waiting is always hard, but God knew best. She would be patient.

One thing was sure. Through all the years to be, she would never regret that her dear lost love, the man whose very faults were dearer to her than another man's virtues, had told her that in very truth he loved her. That knowledge would always be to her sweet store of comfort. It would always seem to give her a sacred right in all his fortunes, a right to set his name in her prayers, to weary Heaven with calling down blessings on his head.

If she heard the world blame him, that, too, would not matter. The one thought, "He loved me," would be as a cloak to cover all his failings; the answering thought, "I loved him," would take possession of him, faults and all; not another, but Lance— Lance, just as he was.

Alison believed that this sweet yet troublous secret of hers was her own and his. She had no fear of prying eyes, of insidious suggestion. She could conjure up no Modred, like a vile reptile crawling on the wall, only fit to be seized and cast forth, as we cast forth the noisome refuse that offends us. As she did towards all men, so gave she credit to all men for doing towards herself, and the very atmosphere in which she had been reared of itself bred an unsuspecting faith in the truth and goodness of all around her.

How healthy, happy, pure and free had been the days of her childhood—the sunny morning of her girlhood! Like some fair flower that has grown in the sheltered nook of a beautiful old *plaisaunce,* she had attained to the full blossom of womanhood knowing neither storm nor tempest; but now the rain of tears was upon her, the tempest of suffering shook her, bowing her down even to the ground. In a few short hours the whole world had been changed to Alison Darling, and she looked back upon the girl of yesterday as we look back upon the days of our lost youth, as we dream of the music that shall sound for us no more. The quiet Sunday-evening hours, always spent by father and daughter in "mamma's room," always hallowed by sweet and noble service of love,

hours of which the language ran, "You cannot be with us through the day; we conse-
crate ourselves, our hearts, our thoughts, our
voices to you now"—these too were fraught
with a new pain. Alison was afraid—afraid
of herself; and fear was a new emotion to
her brave young heart. In the hush and the
stillness of eventide the voice of her heart
rose high, and cried—

"If it felt like this to have lost Lance for
hardly more than four-and-twenty hours; if
this passion of longing crept over her, clutching
her thus cruelly, how should she live through
her life without him? Where was the calm
faith, the resignation of the night before?"

Alison had yet to learn that even to the
holiest soul the hour of turbulence and bitter
rebellion inevitably comes; has to be waded
through, as the tossing surf that leads to the
fair haven of a peaceful and fragrant shore.

Then there was the pain of concealment.
Her life had hitherto been like clear, shining
water, laughing onwards in the sunshine, but
now it had grown turbulent, and sought the

shadow and the shelter of the underwood; the lips that pressed her mother's cheek had known the sweet eagerness of a lover's kiss, and that mother did not know. Love, that to other women meant a crown of pride and rejoicing, to her meant only something to be hidden; no shameful thing, indeed, but something that must be worn as we wear a relic, hidden in our breasts—not like a jewel, held up to the light of day to show to all men its brightness and its beauty. She was defrauded of her woman's diadem; and yet, better this little fragment of the life of Lance Peyton, better those one or two hours of bitter-sweet, under the arching trees and in the rose-garden with him, than a whole lifetime with another man. With such sweet unreasonableness did Alison love the lover who was, as it were, hers but for a moment.

"Is Alison going to sing for me to-night?" said Mrs. Darling, somewhat fretful, perhaps, after a day of more than usual suffering.

"Not to-night, mamma," said the Rector promptly. "The church was—I am sure

I hardly know why—rather close this afternoon, and the child looked tired after service. I shouldn't wonder if Jonathan Straw has been trying a little of his amateur tinkering at the hot-water pipes. You remember when he mended old Sally's washing-copper, and it never held water again? Anyway, I heard an odd sort of fizzing sound once or twice, and the heat seemed to come out in puffs. I must see about it to-morrow. I was about to mention the matter to Westerton, but he slid out of the vestry like a shadow—on tea and toast intent, I doubt not. Jonathan, too, was invisible. Ah! yes, 'conscience doth make cowards of us all.' I doubt not he had been meddling, and, realising that the result was doubtful, did not wish to discuss matters."

"Are you tired, child?" said Mrs. Darling, peering round anxiously at Alison, who sat on a low stool by her side.

"A little, mamma; just a little."

"It is not like you to be tired—it is very odd."

That is the worst of being a healthy and active person ; no one ever expects you to be otherwise.

"Well, well," said the Rector, "a night's rest will set all to rights ; and now, instead of music to-night, I am going to read aloud to you both."

"It will only be another kind of music," put in Alison, with a sly, loving smile.

"Flatterer," returned the Rector, with a droll wave of the hand, "avaunt!"

These two had got into a way of sparring to amuse "Mamma" that had in it something wonderfully touching. There had been times of deep anxiety on her account, when they had gone through quite little performances, helped—ah me!—by the bright boy Cyril— times when to conceal their fears and trouble about her had been part of the cure pre- scribed ; the cheerfulness that doctors occa- sionally order to be taken like a pill or a potion, and that it is sometimes so difficult to make up.

Hence the habit of repartee and gentle

jesting that had grown with the years, the droll saying of this or that village worthy, hoarded up for the "evening hour," the quaint conceit culled from this source or from that, and laid by until that magic time.

But quips and cranks were silent now, and the Rector's wonderful bell-like melodious voice, that people said ought one day to be heard in a cathedral, rolled out the poetry that his soul loved best—

> "A still, small voice spake unto me :
> 'Thou art so full of misery,
> Were it not better not to be?'"

Little he deemed what an echo the words found in a hot, beating heart close by his side.

Was it worth while to live with this dull aching at her heart, with this bitter longing that should know no earthly close?

The mellow voice went on—

> "Then to the still small voice I said :
> 'Let me not cast in endless shade
> What is so wonderfully made.'"

The rest and the tenderness of the beautiful

home-life, the voices of Nature that are the music of God, the divine gift of sympathy that permeates the world, so that to clasp the burning hand and cool the fevered brow brings peace and joy to him that gives, and who, in so giving, is so blest—do these things all count for nothing? Because the one joy is denied, must we then be blind to all about us that is so " wonderfully made " ?

God forbid!

It was well that Alison's face was in the shadow, outside the disc of the shaded lamp, for a crystal tear, and then another and another, gathered and dropped down.

As for the Rector, he was too much absorbed in his book to see anything else.

In the end, the mood of turbulence and rebellion was washed away, and Alison's heart came to her again as the heart of a little child.

Before long the Rectory-house was still and silent. A silver radiance of moonlight flooded its gables and kissed its windows, so that the pigeons cooed in their dovecots, and the

sparrows in the massed ivy gave a faint
twitter now and then.

Alison was sleeping softly, and the moonlight climbed to her face, kissing that too,
and finding the glitter of tears on her eyelids,
but a little smile upon her lips.

The day following, just when the white
evening mist began to creep up from the
Meadows and the daylight began to pale, an
urgent message came from the Old Hall to
the Rectory :—

"Would Mr. Darling go and see Sir
Marmaduke as quickly as might be? Sir
Marmaduke was unwell, or would himself
have waited upon the Rector."

Such messages were not uncommon ; so this
one startled no one.

CHAPTER VIII.

THE RECTOR IS INTERVIEWED.

SIR MARMADUKE PEYTON was undergoing an unpleasant experience. Of course we all feel an absolute and withering contempt for what is called an " anonymous letter." We all say we throw aside and take no notice of such things ; but it is a scorpion that stings sometimes, for all that, and will rankle all the more because we have no visible foe to vent our spleen upon.

The lord of the Old Hall had then received such an epistle. His sense of dignity and of the fitness of things was thereby wounded, as well as his rancour raised by the contents of the same. That any one should dare to discuss his family affairs was intolerable enough; that the innuendoes in the vile scrawl in question should have any foundation in truth, that was beyond endurance. It could not be that there were those in the world resolved to set him at defiance, to plot and plan, to creep about and undermine him!

This was the morbid and exaggerated way in which he put things to himself. He almost had a vague idea of the sin that plots against the "Lord's anointed"—so had the fanaticism that eats the soul preyed upon his nature, warping and deforming all power of seeing things clearly and healthfully.

The obnoxious letter was spread forth upon a table, a letter-weight keeping it down as though it were some noxious insect caught and transfixed. Sir Marmaduke, hollow-eyed, haggard, worn, yet with shining eyes showing brightly under their deep sockets and heavy brows, waited for the Rector. The last few months had been a time of desperate worry and carking anxiety, the marks of the struggle were to be plainly seen, and Sir Marmaduke was evidently what the servants called "not himself." Indeed, had the truth been known, he had not closed his eyes throughout all the long watches of the night, and the unwelcome letter, coming as it did upon a strained and shattered condition of nerves, went near to overset him altogether. There had been, overnight, a long and stormy interview between father and son, then hasty preparations for a journey; and Lance, white and desperate, with all the life in his face concentrated in his burning miserable eyes, had taken a hurried leave of Lady Peyton, while "Mr. Jennings," shaken out of all dignity, grumbled loudly to the footman as the cherished bays had to "step out" to the nearest station—which, indeed, could hardly be called near at all, but was a matter of "miles, and plenty of 'em," as the irate coachman observed, "and no time given to make the critters fit to be seen."

Lance gone, Sir Marmaduke appeared to be somewhat easier. His spirits always rose during those times (of late neither few nor far between) when his son was away from the Hall, and a silence reigned supreme over all— such a silence as, Mrs. Dutton declared, " got

into her ears and buzzed like bees! and, oh,
me! for the good old days that were gone,
when Master Cyril sang about the old place,
and was always at his nonsense with 'dear
old Dutty.'"

As has been said already, it was towards
the afternoon of that fateful Monday that Sir
Marmaduke's message reached the Rectory,
while the Rector, gracefully yielding, not unpleasantly, to a sort of gentle "Monday lassitude," not uncommon with the country clergy,
was smoking the pipe of peace, while Alison
read aloud to him a book just then much talked
of.   He was resting on his oars a while before
starting on a long trudge to visit a sick man
in a far outlying hamlet, and Alison had just
declared her intention of going too, with a
basket of good things for the sufferer, when
the message from the Hall arrived.

"Dear me!" said Mrs. Darling when they
told her, " I hope Sir Marmaduke is not ill—or,
that there is any bad news about Cyril?"

"God forbid!" said the Rector fervently.
"I see no reason to fear such calamity; it is

much more likely that he wants another
argument with me as to the Romanising
tendency of Alison's new altar-cloth," and
Mr. Darling looked as though it would have
done him good to have made a wry face, as
children do at the prospect of a dose. Those
terrible " arguments " with Sir Marmaduke—
when the talking was all on one side, and the
wildest theories of fanaticism flung at the
Rector's head made him feel dazed and almost
ready to lose patience with a misguided man,
and let his temper run away with him—were
sore trials, though they might be wholesome
ones.

Alison ran to get the brush and brush off
any specks of dust that might obscure the
spotless black of the Rector's coat, Mrs.
Darling looking on from her couch with a
satisfied smile.

It pleased her to see Alison fill her place
so well; to see the ready, willing hands offer
all those little services of love that she herself
was helpless to perform. And, indeed, it
may be said that the Rector was kept what is

called "spick and span," and no mistake, and
made as spruce as a new pin in every point of
his clerical armour at all times.

But Alison's hands trembled now as she held
the brush, and she was glad to hide her face
by bending over her work.

Was that blessed " chance " of which Lance
had spoken about to shine out like a sun and
brighten all the world of her heart and hopes ?
Would her father see Lance ? would—— But
no ; she was losing herself—losing her head
in speculations, fancyings, idle imaginations.
In all probability some parish business (did
not Sir Marmaduke love to put a disturbing
finger in every parish pie ?) was at the bottom
of this hurried summons. She was busy with
a rather difficult bit of translation of one of
Lessing's plays ; she would go and plunge
into it ; try to forget herself and her bewilder-
ments, and surprise her father with a charming bit of composition when their next
" German hour " together should come.

No sooner had the Rector been ushered
into the oak-room, and taken one quiet com-

prehensive glance at his host's face, than he
realised the fact that in the present case
parish affairs were assuredly not to be the
subject under discussion. No difficulties about
choir or altar trappings, no wish to tear to
tatters this or that opinion unfolded in the
pulpit where contradiction was impossible
and the matter had to be fought out at a
more convenient season, would make a man's
hand not only cold but tremulous, or fill a
man's eyes with such a light of passionate
revolt.

On his part, Sir Marmaduke, waving his
visitor to a seat, wished that the Rector of
Scarsdale had been any other than the man
he was.

As he fidgeted about a moment among
his papers before himself taking a seat, his
thoughts ran—somewhat erratically, it must
be confessed—upon "that ass Westerton,"
whom he could have "crumpled up in a
moment, shrivelled into mere touch-paper,
bless you! with a breath." But there sat the
Rev. Reginald Wentworth Darling, not in the

least looking like a man either to be crumpled
up or shrivelled into touch-paper; indeed,
Sir Marmaduke felt that he had never before
thoroughly realised the height, and breadth of
shoulder, for which the Rector of Scarsdale
was remarkable. It seemed as if in the grey
and silvery light that gleamed in through the
high-arched window Mr. Darling's proportions
grew before the eyes of the man who watched
him, and the glance, quiet, steadfast, gently
inquiring, became harder and harder to meet.
Nothing could be more courtly than the outward manner and demeanour of Sir Marmaduke in this crisis; inwardly he was fuming
and chafing at a growing sense of inferiority
and a maddening feeling of hesitation—one
might almost call it shyness—that paralysed
his will, and crept over him as the mesmeric
influence creeps over a helpless "subject."
He had intended to plunge *in medias res;*
had, indeed, pinned down the obnoxious letter
—for he felt its loathsomeness even while he
permitted it to disturb and torture him—as a
scientist might pin down a specimen round

which the storm of discusssion was about to
rage.

Instead, however, of flying at the specimen,
clutching it, as it were, and thrusting it into
the face of the meeting, Sir Marmaduke, quite,
as it appeared to him, in spite of very different resolves, opened the engagement—for
it was bound to be that—thus :—

"The days lengthen out wonderfully, do
they not?"

The Rector wondered within himself if he
had been summoned in such urgent fashion to
discuss the weather, the time of year, and
such-like kindred topics; but as he glanced
keenly at his companion's face, he recognised
the signs of some deep inward trouble—some
ruffling of the usually stolid composure. He
moved in his chair, throwing one arm across
the back, and so turning to face the baronet
more fully.

"Yes," he said, "they do indeed, and the
added hours of daylight are pleasant to me,
especially since I am, as you know, a great
pedestrian."

Then silence, during which an uneasy movement of the foot in Sir Marmaduke, and perfect stillness and repose on the part of the
Rector.

Hound, lying crouched upon the rug, rose,
stretched himself, and looked from one to the
other, as who should say, " What a couple of
numskulls you are, sitting mumchance like
that ! "

Then something in the Rector's face at-
tracted him ; he lurched across the room, and
laid his great head on the arm of the black
clerical coat ; not unnoticed either, you may
be sure, yet caressed in a somewhat absent
manner, for Mr. Darling was mentally and
bodily in an attitude of waiting. He was
conscious of that peculiar sensation well described as " feeling thunder in the air ;" nor
did he fail to note the tremble of the fine,
long-fingered hand, with its one massive crest-
ring, of the man opposite to him.

At last that hand was passed slowly and
lingeringly over Sir Marmaduke's mouth, as
if to steady the lips for the utterance of

certain words that appeared to come un-
readily.

"Mr. Darling, I have been very much
annoyed—I may say most deeply, most intensely annoyed—to-day."

The Rector bowed.

Was he going to be called upon to adjudi-
cate between two opponents, and if so, what
was the ground of dispute?

He earnestly hoped it was no question of
dogma—no correspondence upon free will,
predestination, assurance of salvation, or the
worthlessness of good deeds done by one
outside the peculiar pale which it pleased Sir
Marmaduke to call "the fold." Such topics,
and others akin to them, had been thrust
under his unwilling notice too often; never,
however, with the effect of luring him into
actual controversy. That the gentleman opposite looked upon him as an individual far
removed from a "state of grace," and as an
alien from that very limited fold in which the
collection of sheep was so small and so select,
Mr. Darling well knew. He was resigned to

the position, and calm under the verdict.
The question, however, that now presented
itself to his mind was, could this interview
mean an attack on the old ground—the Sunday's sermon—or was it something new?

"I am sorry you have been annoyed."

"The cause of that annoyance is a most
singular letter which I received this morning."

"Is it the personality of Satan, or the
eternity of punishment?" thought the Rector,
restraining a little squirm of impatience and
repulsion with some difficulty, and reasoning
for the present from the past.

"A most unpleasant thing has happened
to me," went on the Baronet, after a short
and uneasy pause; "some one—it may be
with good intentions; we are distinctly told
not to judge—has sent me an anonymous
letter."

"There can be no such things as good
intentions in the matter of a letter of that
base kind. It is always a stab in the dark,
always the most pitiful and detestable weapon
a cowardly hand can use."

The Rector's voice had a ring that his companion did not like. Tyranny almost always runs in double harness with fanaticism—as witness all the cruelties done in the name of religion. Sir Marmaduke did not relish the feeling that the spirit of opposition was in the air. He had a grave grievance, and he wanted to air it, and to see the opposing forces fall prostrate at the sound of his battle-cry.

He unpinned the specimen—in other words, lifted the weight from the prostrate letter, and handed the paper, with a courtly bow, in which lurked no little malice and triumph, to the Rector.

Anything more absolutely unsuspicious than the frame of mind in which that good man settled his *pince-nez* on his handsome nose and commenced to read the precious effusion can hardly be conceived. As he read on a crimson flush mounted to the roots of his hair, and his hand clenched upon the paper.

Not one of these signs was lost upon the

man who watched. In the littleness and narrowness of his own stunted mind he looked upon these as the emotions roused by baulked design and ambition thwarted.

Mr. Darling read on and on, word by word, line by line, taking in all the mean innuendo, the insulting suggestion, that lurked beneath them.

He was so long silent that the other became impatient. Was this silence the confusion of detected guilt or the dogged resolve to hold on to the advantage he supposed himself to have gained by his daughter's intrigue with the heir of the Old Hall?

Sir Marmaduke called it an "intrigue" in his own mind, because he wanted to think of it in the most offensive way possible. It pleased him to use such expressions to himself, as tending to give vent to the resentment within him. Not that he did not recognise the worth, womanliness, and beauty of Alison Darling, but because just now she was presented to his mind as an obstacle to his own will, a stumbling-block to the fulfilment of his own ambitions and desires. Therefore he was unjust and cruel.

The Rector was struggling with himself. He would not speak until he had got himself well in hand. If he had said all he thought and felt, heaven only knows what would have been the result. He had grown as white as he was flushed before. His hand, letter and all, had fallen to his knee.

"It is a woman," he said, "if one does not prostitute that holy name to call her so who can thus write of another woman."

This was not what Sir Marmaduke had expected the Rector to say—not at all. For a moment he was nonplussed.

"It may be well-intentioned."

The letter was crushed into a ball, and flung aside like an asp. There it lay, a blotch of white on the tapestry carpet. There it had to lie, for Sir Marmaduke instinctively felt that to follow and stoop to pick it up would be stooping indeed.

"Believe me, my dear sir," began Sir Marmaduke suavely, thinking it best to temporise with the enemy, who certainly looked unpleasantly combative—" believe me, I fully recognise and—ahem !—enter into the force of the—er—temptation."

" To what ? "

How high the Rector's head was held ! how his clear blue eyes—so like, yet just then so unlike, Alison's—blazed and shone out defiance ! It really made it very difficult for Sir Marmaduke, the man taking it in that way.

" Well—er—the advantages, mere worldly advantages, I grant, dross—dross ; still, the position in the future—the fact of Lance being my eldest son——"

" Sir Marmaduke, I pity you ; I do indeed. I pity you from the bottom of my heart."

The evident sincerity of these words made them hit all the harder. The reply came sharply—

" And may I ask why ? "

" I pity you to think that you can look in my daughter's face and believe her, even for a passing moment, capable of such mean, such

despicable motives as those you are ready to
impute to her. Believe me, I knew nothing
of this matter when I entered your presence
this evening; I know no more now than what
you have shown me; but I will stake my
word, my honour, my reputation as a minister
of God, against my dear girl's womanliness,
her stainless truth, her absolute loyalty, and
perfect maidenliness. She never, in all her
pure young life, made what that villainous
document calls an 'assignation' with any
man."

"Her interview with my son seems, at all
events, to have been of a peculiar and agitating
nature," answered Sir Marmaduke.

"May be! I have never pried into the
secrets of my daughter's life. If there were
anything she wished to tell me, she would
have done so, and your son, Sir Marmaduke,
your son—when has he been anything but an
honourable gentleman?"

"Still men are weak where women are concerned. I am worldling enough to know that,
Mr. Darling, and there is no reason to suppose

my son an exception to an almost universal rule. I regret to say that I have never discerned in him any decided signs of the working of grace."

"Pardon me," said the Rector, with a dignified gesture of the hand, "I am not here to discuss the spiritual condition of your son, but an impropriety, an unseemliness, of which you dare to accuse my daughter."

"Dare, Mr. Darling?"

"Yes, dare! If some skulking idiot met my girl walking with her old companion and playfellow; if the person in question noticed that she was agitated, tearful—what you will—why should you so misjudge one of whom you have never known anything but good as to brand her as designing and unmaidenly?"

Sir Marmaduke felt that things were really becoming very unpleasant, and he always *had* objected to that habit of the Rector's when agitated of pacing up and down the room like a caged animal in its den. Hound, too, took to pacing up and down alongside Mr.

Darling, every now and then looking up
gravely into his face.

How can you fix a person with your glittering eye when he is conducting himself like a
sort of human pendulum? How can you be
impressive, scathing, witheringly majestic,
when the point you aim at is a moving and
mutable one?

"I have never stated that Miss Darling was
unmaidenly," said the Baronet, taking up a
silver-hilted paper-knife, and trifling with it,
to give himself countenance.

"You have inferred it," replied the peri-
patetic Rector; "and I repeat again that I
cannot allow the slightest slur to rest upon
the purity of her motives or her conduct."

"I have not the remotest intention of——"

"Sir Marmaduke," said the Rector, standing, tall and stern and big, right in front of
the Baronet, "permit me to say that you
have taken—at all events to my mind—a
very strange course of conduct in this matter.
Would it not have been the better way to
have spoken out at once to your son? Nay,

I may be wronging you. Perhaps you have already taken this course. If so, may I beg of you most earnestly to deal candidly—absolutely candidly—with me, as between man and man? In place of hints and innuendoes, give me facts to deal with."

Looking up at the towering form and resolute face, one insistent thought kept recurring to Sir Marmaduke's mind—

" If it were Westerton now——"

But it was not Westerton, and it was utterly futile to give a thought to the process called " crumpling up," or anything of that nature.

A stubborn fact in the shape of the Rev. Reginald Wentworth Darling had to be reckoned with. With his own hands Sir Marmaduke had roused the lion, and the animal had now to be wrestled with. The owner of the Old Hall was no coward, and rose to the situation.

" I never even hinted to my son that I had received "—here he gave a somewhat rueful glance at the crushed-up ball of paper

on the carpet—" I never once hinted to him,
I say, that such a communication had been
made to me."

"Sir Marmaduke!" broke in the Rector,
but the other bowed and hurried on.

" In truth, I could not have spoken upon
such a subject to my son, because, had I
done so, I should have insulted a lady for
whom I have the deepest, the most profound
regard—the Lady Jane Kynaston, to whom
my son is affianced."

The Rector flushed a deep red, the hands
at his sides closed and unclosed as those of
one in some overpowering agony.

His Alison, his little girl, the creature
whom he had watched over and guarded as
the precious gift of Heaven! What awful
sorrow was this that had come upon her—
a sorrow so deep and so hopeless, that she
had hoarded it away from the one to whom
she ought most eagerly to have turned?

Even as he stood there, silent, because
only so could his indignation be kept within
due bounds, even then the echo of her voice

the day before seemed to reach his strained
ear—her voice, which had been to him almost
as the voice of a stranger, thrilled through
and through as it was with a passion and
pain unknown before—

> " If Thou should'st call me to resign
> What most I prize—it ne'er was mine—
> I only yield Thee what is Thine.
> Thy will be done ! "

His darling—his own little girl! she was
laying her gift upon the altar, opening her
hand wide that God might take from her
even what He willed ; and she had borne it
all in silence—she had let the fire consume
her heart and uttered no word !

A hot impulse was on him to rush out
and away among the shadows of evening
that were gathering over dale and hill—away
to find her, clasp her, comfort her.

An odd, incongruous vision of her in the
far past came over him, as such things do
at strange, unseemly times.

A bee had stung her—she a toddling wee
bit lassie " rising four ; " and she came to

him across the grass, her big sun-bonnet
falling back upon her shoulders, the glory
of her golden hair falling about her face.
She was holding out the swollen hand, looking at it with wide eyes and a quivering
lip.

"The bee have stung mine ickle hand,
daddy dear; but me no cry."

It was the same old story—"me no cry."

Like the lightning flash these thoughts
passed through the Rector's mind.

Sir Marmaduke was looking steadily out
of the window, where the mist was seen
creeping up over the lawn, and touching
the lowermost sweeping boughs of the great
cedars. He looked a calm, contemplative
figure; he might have been taken for a
model of the high-bred county gentleman,
whose lineage runs back as deeply into the
past as the roots of the great trees upon his
lands into the earth. But any one going
close up to him would have noted the
shimmer of a dank sweat upon his brow
where the fine curled hair was slightly worn

away and grey above the temples, and the knuckles stood out white upon the hand that grasped the arm of his chair.

He was playing a desperate game, and he knew it; but the stakes were high and the risks worth the running.

Like most of the men who take refuge later on in life in a violent fanaticism, of what nature soever it may be, there had been a time, now very far back, it is true, but still there in memory and result—the time of a stormy youth. Of late a spectre, gaunt and threatening, had reared its ugly head from the grave of time, and stared Sir Marmaduke in the eyes, holding out a claw-like skeleton hand to clutch. All was at stake. Name, position, the credit of the narrow and bigoted creed that, poor a thing as it may seem to us, was yet dear to the misguided heart and blinded eyes—blinded to the loving and universal fatherhood of God.

This man was no hypocrite; he believed that he believed all the fearsome tenets of an exploded creed, and if a certain love of money,

not so much for what it could procure, but as
money *per se*, mingled with the doctrine of a
special predestination and the sinfulness of
all things fair and beautiful in Nature, he
was no wonderful exception; for greed and
bigotry run ofttimes hand-in-hand, and those
who would never sin with the hands will sin
with the tongue when material advantage is
concerned. With Sir Marmaduke, indeed, the
case was desperate; and desperate remedies
were called for. Desperate remedies always
mean that some one must be sacrificed, and
Lance had been the victim.

"Since your son is, as you say, affianced to
Lady Jane Kynaston, what do you suppose
is the state of things between him and my
daughter? What, in a word, have you sent
for me here to say to me?"

The Rector by this time had himself well
in hand. He realised that the battle must be
fought warily, and with a cool head.

"I take it," said Sir Marmaduke, joining
his shapely hands carefully finger to finger,
and watching the process intently, "that

there has been a sentimental attachment, a foolish, reckless sort of shilly-shallying going on, unknown to you, and to my wife and myself."

"I think we had better leave Lady Peyton out of the question," said the Rector sternly ; "she would never countenance any such accusation against Alison as that you made a while back."

" Indeed, I make no accusation," said the other suavely. "Youth is youth."

"Quite so; but there is no need for youth to be dishonourable. My daughter would never act in the way attributed to her. Sir Marmaduke, there is some simple explanation of the facts stated in that vile communication —if facts they are."

"I have placed the matter in your hands," said Sir Marmaduke with a wave of the hand that might have done credit to some great diplomatic question. "I have confided to you the position in which my son stands towards the family of my old friend Lord Kynaston. As I told you before, I fully realise the temptation—I will be candid, and say the temptation on both sides. Alison is a most attractive girl. The position and fortune of my son——"

" Silence ! " thundered the Rector. " I will not hear one word more. If, as you say, your son is affianced to Lady Jane Kynaston, his name must not be for a moment connected with that of my daughter. Bear in mind also, Sir Marmaduke, there might be other matters than this 'sentimental attachment' you are so ready to presuppose, which might have caused the agitation alluded to in that scurrilous and cowardly document there. It is possible that Lance might have had a letter from our dear Cyril, he who is so dear to us, and is so sorely missed."

" No, no ; nothing of the kind—nothing of the kind, I assure you. I should have known —I should have known——"

Here Sir Marmaduke began to fuss and fidget among his many papers, and the grey light from the window above shone pale on his set and chiselled face.

"You wish me to understand that this interview is at an end?" said the Rector. He still kept complete control over himself, but his eyes were not pleasant to meet, and therefore Sir Marmaduke avoided them.

"Yes, I have letters to see to. I feel that now I have — in confidence — put you in possession of certain facts, you will see that any folly in the past——"

"There has been no folly in the past," put in the Rector resolutely.

"Good! have it as you will," replied the other. "At all events, you will agree with me that all ambitious hopes——"

"There have been no ambitious hopes."

"Good again! At all events, permit me to say, and permit me to feel that we understand each other."

"And your son? Can I see him? Perhaps, indeed, that would have been the most straightforward way at the first."

The grey light no longer shone upon a pale and chiselled face; rather it showed one flushed, working, wrathful, with eyes that flashed and burned.

"My son left for London early this morning ; my son knows nothing—absolutely nothing— of this—this affair ; he is gone to be the guest of Lord Kynaston."

"As the acknowledged suitor of the Lady Jane ? "

"As one whom I know to be welcome to the Kynaston family in such a relationship. I can, however, hardly say 'acknowledged suitor,' since it was but this morning that he openly declared to me his own feeling on the subject."

But even as he spoke, might it not well have been that some memory should have haunted him — some memory of a dark haggard face, of a weary, desperate man, yielding up his own will at last under the spur of a revelation, unlooked for, heart-rending, terrible alike to speaker and hearer? Some memory of a parting without a word of farewell; of a promise given with white lips, with miserable eyes that stared at nothing, as though on the empty air they saw limned the face of a woman loved and sad, weariful, lost, hopeless as his own ?

"Papa, do not speak to me so tenderly. You will make me cry, and then mamma will see and know. Oh, dear papa, this sorrow must be kept between us two; we must bear it as we can, and live it down for her sake! It was as I have told you; it came all in a moment. I do not think he meant it, nor did I; it was like a flash. And now forgive me—oh, forgive me!—that I have brought such trouble on your loving heart—your loving, tender heart! He loves me—Lance loves me—indeed he does. He has loved me, not knowing, all the years—as I him. I did not know why he said that we must part, but now I understand. He was bound already, bound in honour. We cannot tell, we cannot judge, how he drifted into that; but if I, out of my aching heart, can quite forgive him, as I do, dear, as I do—then you can pardon him too, and we can pray—can pray——"

Her voice faltered, trembled, strangled, broke. She threw up her arms, and he caught her and held her close, laying his hand upon her bowed head as though he would fain have shielded her from all harm.

But she shed no tear. It was the old story of the bee that stung the pink-palmed, chubby little hand, "Me no cry—me no cry."

Thus Alison faced her sorrow, bearing it all the better because she had learnt the divine lesson of setting another before herself.

"I will tell you all about it, papa," she said, lifting her pure pale face to his. "He asked me to forgive him; he called himself hard and bitter names for having uttered words he had no right to say; and then he kissed me—such a 'kiss good-bye,' papa! All the rest are hers—hers always; but that was mine—is mine—always will be mine, won't it, dear? And there is something else that I must tell you—something very, very precious—most precious, I think, of all. He said that I had helped him, strengthened him,

comforted him many, many times   Was not
that sweet to hear?"

The man was greatly moved.   She felt the
arms that held her tremble; she saw, with a
sort of terror, that he watched her through
welling tears—he so great, so grand, so
calm!

"Ah! do not be so sorry," she cried, stroking the hand that lay upon her shoulder;
"do not be so sad.   You have always told
me that God's love shines brightest for us
when we are in sorrow.   He will not desert
me now.   Perhaps it wasn't much of a time
I had—not very long counted by minutes;
but it was a sweet little time—a dear little
time before the sadness of it came; and we
thought that no one would ever know.   Papa,
I shall always love the rose-garden best of all,
the place where he took such piteous leave of
me, where he said 'God bless you.   Oh, my
dear lost love, God bless you all day and
every day!'   Papa, do not look like that; I
tell you I can bear it.   I am quite brave;
indeed I am.   Hush! that is mamma calling;

let us go to her.   No, I will go; you had
better wait a wee, dear."

But he held her back a moment.

"Alison," he said, and his voice was hoarse,
and shook, "try to remember; did you meet
any one that day when you walked with
Lance beside the Falls?"

"No one," she said.   "At least, yes—oh, I
remember now—Mr. Westerton."

Then, with a muttered word—a hard word
to pass those kindly lips—he let her go.

CHAPTER IX.

"THE BEST LAID SCHEMES OF MICE
AND MEN . . ."

THE rich marriage about to be made by Sir
Marmaduke Peyton's elder son was soon the
general topic of conversation in Scarsdale.
All mention of "retrenchment" at the Old
Hall was dropped "like a hot potato," as
the Australian gentleman's daughter put it
tersely, and everybody said to everybody else
that the Peytons were decidedly "in luck,"
for Lady Jane would have a dower of fifty
thousand pounds at the least, and, besides
(so some friend of the Kynaston family had
said), she was over head and ears in love
with Launcelot Peyton, and positively insisted upon only a part of the sum above
named being settled upon herself and possible
children.

Sir Marmaduke seemed to have taken a new lease of life. His *malaise* disappeared as if by the touch of a magic wand, and those long seclusions in the library which had so disturbed the peaceful routine of the household were gradually discontinued, until, as Mrs. Dutton had it, "Master was himself again—praise be!—and had begun to get over the parting with the sweetest young gentleman that ever lived, precious Master Cyril."

Then Dutton shook her head and made hopeless gestures with her hands.

"As for my lady, I really do believe and estimate as she'll go moanin' all her days, with no comfort except to talk to Hound when they two are together by their own selves, which I've heard her many and many's the time, and it's dreadful upsettin', too, to have a party talking to a heathen dog same as if he was a Christian. It's enough to upset a saint, as the sayin' goes; which I never was a saint, nor never look to be, so it may be well supposed I'm left without a

leg to stand on when I see Hound lookin'
for all the world just as if he knew every
word my Lady says, and putting on a face
as much as to say, 'We're very busy, Mrs.
Dutton, the two of us, havin' a talk about
Master Cyril, and please go away and don't
interrupt us.'"

"I dunna believe you, mum," said a yokel
from the stable, scratching his head as if to
stimulate his brains. "I dunna believe the
dawg ever said a bloomin' wurred."

"In course he didn't," replied Mrs. Dutton
with contempt; "that's what they call an
image, that is; but you've no more head
than a button turnip."

"If yo' was a makin' things up same as
the story-books, missis, why didn't you say
so? Yo' give me a rum start, any way,
for I'd a moind t' think the dwag wur took
in hydrostatics, and 'ud ha' to be shot or
summat, and I would'na loike to see 'im
made away wi' atwixt two feather-beds, nor
nowt o' that sort, for Maister Cyril he
thought a lot o' him, he did, an' there's but

one moind among the lot on us about Maister Cyril, and that's all about it. We've a moind to think t' ould place has never bin t' same sin' he went for a sodger, nor never will be more till he sets foot in it agen, an' cheers t' lot on us wi' t' soight o' his bonnie face."

The voice of that yokel might have been taken for that of all Scarsdale, to say nothing of the county round. Who did not miss the cheery-hearted blithe young fellow with his laughing eyes and his winsome smile? What gathering could take place without some one saying, with a sigh, "How one does miss Cyril Peyton!"

It is a grand thing to be great; it is a noble thing to be distinguished, learned, wise; but it is also a sweet thing to be greatly loved, just as the birds and flowers, the sunlit sky, and the blue rippling sea are loved because they are so fair to see, and help to make life beautiful and bright. Certainly Lance was not likely to make up to any one for the loss of Cyril. Deeper and deeper seemed to grow the gloom that

at times overshadowed him, while something
very like estrangement appeared to have
come about between himself and his father.
People said that Lady Jane would have to
put forth all her wiles to cheer this dark-
faced lover of hers. Some (in the village)
spoke with bated breath of the witch's curse;
and Mother Bond, who grew madder every
day, was more and more shunned and feared.
There were, indeed, not wanting some who
endeavoured to propitiate the goddess, as
men of old tried to bribe the spirits of the
woods and fields. Fruit and vegetables—
even chickens and eggs—would be laid on
her doorstep overnight by invisible hands:
a grey homespun cloak was made for her,
and hung on a tree hard by, and great was
the universal joy when she appeared clad in
its warm folds, and the hood thereof, that
had been fashioned with much subtlety and
care, drawn over her tangled head. From
this shelter her eerie face, with all its life
concentrated in the bright piercing grey eyes,
that could — so said Scarsdale — look you

through and through, and take note of all your thoughts and notions, same as if they were written in a book, looked curiously at the passers-by, ever seeking, never finding, the thing they sought. She would sit crouched at the gateway, plaiting straws—(tradition had it she had been a bonnet-maker in her youth, and came from some distant village with the brat on her back who afterwards became the mother of Danny)—yet always what is called "on the listen," letting her hands fall into her lap as she heard a footstep. Some day, some day, Danny would come running down the lane, across the bridge, on and on, and then in at the little gate. She must wait—wait—wait. No one waited for ever.

Sometimes she stopped a passer-by, and asked, "Ha' yo' seen my boy Danny?" And being told (in fear and trembling, expectant of a curse) that no such person had been seen that day, would go in quickly to her tumbledown abode, and beat on the wall with fierce spasmodic hands, until the blood

started to the palms and the nails grew
livid and torn, the while the villager would
make him or herself scarce with surprising
rapidity, being, indeed, out of sight before a
person could say "knife."

The more venturesome would talk to her
sometimes.

"He's gone for to be a sodger," they would
say; "and one day he'll come up the road,
beatin' a little drum, wi' a red coat on's back,
and a little 'at wi' a gold button i' front—
that'll be Danny."

But the poor dazed mind could not take
it in. Mother Bond would turn a blank
face on the speaker, and make motions with
her hands as if she were strangling some-
body. Then the others would take to rapid
flight. They said the mill-wheel talked to
Mother Bond, and Mother Bond knew what
it said; in truth, heaven knows if the dull
thud and rush of the beaten water and the
thrill and tremble of the mill had not a sooth-
ing charm for the distraught senses!

Anyway, the Scarsdale witch would crawl

down by the bridge, and huddle herself into a certain niche by the low span of the dark archway, and there—a grey-hooded ghost—watch and wait for that which never came. At the bridge-end, at her own gateway, by the mill-wheel, it was always the same watching and waiting—waiting and watching for that which never came.

Nor was hers the only heart that thus kept weary vigil.

Time, whose gentle healing hand softens most sorrows, brought no solace to the heart of Lady Peyton, brought no cessation of the reproaches and taunts that were her daily food. It is hard to judge the fanatic, for, once the moral sense is twisted all askew, who may say what aspect things take?

Did Sir Marmaduke really believe he was scourging a soul for its immortal good as he kept the wound raw that bled for Cyril's loss? Did the Inquisitor of old believe that he was doing God's work as he gave the signal for the strained and tortured limbs to be agonised by yet one more turn of the rack?

These are deep things to try; fanaticism is
a disease of the brain, as madness is; and
who can judge the madman?

As time went on, letters came—not swift-
winged, as in the days in which we now live,
but haltingly, yet full of love and thoughful-
ness for those at home—from Cyril in far
lands. He wrote of Danny, called by general consent "the stowaway," because in that
contraband fashion he had made the voyage
eastward. He had been unearthed like a
fox from its run about midway over ocean,
and cast, a tattered miserable object, at the
feet of the captain of the ship—miserable,
gaunt, tattered, unkempt, but still every inch
Danny Spool, with all the lustre of his native
impudence undimmed. Cyril told in his
letters how the imp had won his way with
every one, and "'listed" almost on the spot,
appearing in gorgeous apparel as if by magic,
and settling down to beat a kettledrum as
though he had never done anything else
through life; turning out also a choice per-
former on the penny-whistle, and a dancer

of the double-shuffle to be excelled by few
or none.

"I come to foller on to Maister Cyril, and
fur to be a sodger same as 'im," was all the
explanation Danny chose to give of his appearance in the midst of a mixed "lot" of men
going from dépôts to headquarters; officers
joining from leave, officers who had never
joined at all, and were on their way to do
it; officers' wives going out from England
to join their husbands in India, and wearing
that eager longing look you may see in the
faces of those who are on their way to meet
all that is dearest to them in all the world;
and men off "furlough," full of yarns of all
they had said and done, and a good deal
they had neither said nor done. Danny was
there, that was enough, in mid-ocean. Some
one, it was not very clear who, had fed him
and tended him when he lay curled up like
a squirrel in a "crafty" corner. Perhaps
suspicion might have pointed to that newly-
enlisted soldier, Private Dorrington, who was
behaving like a saint in the hope of getting

"privilege," and being in the far distant
future an officer's servant; but suspicion
held her tongue.   Drummer Danny was
adopted by the "draft" of men who were
going to join the 97th at Kurrachee, appeared in a "let down" uniform, and im-
mediately saluted as though he had been to
the manner born, quickly acquiring the art
of making his forage-cap hang on, all on
one side, in the miraculous way peculiar
to drummer-boy's caps,—a way that I have
never beheld the head-gear of any other
mortal "conduct."   *En passant*, I may mention that we had a drummer-boy in the dear
old "Two Twos," as the "Cheshire" used to
be called, whose cap beat anything I ever
saw.   We used to suggest cobbler's wax!
Goodness knows how that cap stuck on, but
its knowing "set" well became the blithe
and bonnie young face of the soldier lad—
the blithest, bonniest, merriest grig that
ever beat a drum, and got into endless
scrapes for playing "larks" of all kinds and
descriptions.   He was our "merry-man" for

many a day; sang "The Young Recruit" at
our "Soldiers' Evenings;" and once made a
speech at a tea-party which makes me laugh
now when I think of it. Now he lies sleeping in the cemetery at Guernsey; the blue
bright sea sings his lullaby, and the myriad
blossoms of that island of flowers bloom
above his grave. What memories start to
life as I write!—the beauteous golden morning when I took my way to our hospital
for that solemn rite, the dying boy's last
Communion; the worn face, the hollow cough,
and the one—only one—word of regret: "It
'ull seem strange, ma'am, when the regiment
gets the route, and I've got to be left behind."
A tear stole down the sunken cheek—those
of us who stood round were not in much
better case—and soon, very soon the pet of
the regiment was borne to his last resting-
place, and the sound of the drums and fifes
rang out over the sun-bright sea. I seem to
hear their echo now, which must plead my
excuse for leaving Danny Spool so long on
the deck of the good old troopship, with

Private Dorrington giving a sly eye at his antics, and Ensign Peyton—that gay young fellow whom the whole community already blindly worshipped—passed with a smile that was more precious to Danny than all the gold of the Indies.

Danny himself wrote a letter at last.

It ran thus—

"INDIA.

"DEAR GRANNY,—It be fine to be a sodger. 1 day I'll cum 'ome wi' a gin'ral's 'at on me 'ed.—From yours truly,

'OLE DANNY SPOOL,
As wouldna' go to schule,
His own self.

"Mister Ciril is ere ; 'ee is an hensine."

This epistle was no doubt meant well, and duly directed to—

"MRS. MOTHER BOND,
Lower Scarsdale Village,
(Behint the Mill),
Yorkshire County,
England."

The writing was a hand that was not Danny's, and evidently the somewhat ambitious work of a comrade, for in the corner of the envelope was a fancy sketch of Danny in a general's cocked-hat and feathers, set astride an animal that might have been a cross between a lop-eared rabbit and a donkey; and, as Scarsdale observed—and the oak-tree parliament fully affirmed—Danny had never shown any artistic talent beyond once writing in white chalk across the constable's door an epithet, scathing indeed, but distinctly lacking in propriety, and without pictorial design.

"Yon picter never came out of *his* addle 'ed," said Maister Straw; "it's drawed by a man of parts, that is; and it shows what fine company the varmin's got into. I reckon he looks down on the loikes o' us for a set o' first-class num'yeds by this toime."

"I'd num'yed 'im, if I got 'im," said Pilkington, the lawful apparitor, who had a grudge against Danny. But the others were all on the side of the ne'er-do-weel, and full of admiration of the high company into which he had worked himself.

It may, however, be doubted if the letter thus indited by the talented artist who was a believer in the axiom that the general's baton lurks in the soldier's knapsack was of much comfort to Mother Bond. They took it to her; they read it to her; but they never succeeded in banishing that terrible far-off look from her eager eyes; the words seemed to carry no meaning to her stricken brain. She was, all the time, watching down the road for Danny.

"Hoo' wur allers a bit daft-like, ever sin' the day she come from no man knows wheer, wi' brat on her back, and sot her down by t' bridge, but now hoo's clean daft, and gone beyant reason; an' they do say as Heaven looks kind on them as is that way and ac's up to the curses of 'em. Onyway, I'd a deal liefer ha' a kind wurred than a foul fro' Mother Bond."

Thus ran opinion in Scarsdale, Upper and Lower.

Her Majesty's mails are no respecters of persons, and, check by jowl with the missive for Mother Bond, came a letter from Cyril for his brother Lance. By this time he had heard of the engagement with the Lady Jane. He was surprised—pleased in a way, since those at home were so. Then he went on to say—"Perhaps, dear old fellow, I was wrong to say what I did some time ago about—you know who. I daresay it was all fancy on my part, but it had taken hold of me somehow, and out of the fulness of the heart the mouth —or rather the pen—spake; maybe, too, the wish was father to the thought. You know how I love them all. Ah me! how often I think of the dear old place, the pigeons, the grey chickens fluttering round, greedy little beasts! seeing who could gorge the most grain, and—dear sweet Alison!"

Lance grew very thoughtful over this letter. There was a pucker between his dark eyebrows, a set look about his lips as he read.

"I think foreign mails must be rather

uncertain, mother," he said that night. "I cannot help thinking a letter from the boy must have miscarried somehow—one written a long while back; but when people are at a great distance it is no good trying to set those things straight, is it?"

"Hardly," said Lady Peyton, looking up from her book, so that the light from the high clustered sconces fell full upon her face.

It startled him to see how pale she was. What a look, almost of fear, had come into her eyes!

"I should not have spoken of the boy," he thought. "How sensitive she is! What would become of her if anything——" But even in thought the idea was too dreadful to complete. A new tenderness had sprung up in the heart of Lance Peyton towards his mother since the lines of his own life had run in troubled ways. There is nothing that better teaches us the lesson of sympathy than standing in need of sympathy ourselves, and Lance watched his mother with changed

eyes—eyes that saw many things to which
they had been blind before. Lady Peyton
did not say, and never had said, much to
her son about his engagement to Lady Jane.
She only said, as he bent and kissed her
cheek when first the announcement was made,
"Whoever either of my sons marries will be
as a daughter to me, Lance," and at that he
kissed her hand.

There were moments when Launcelot Peyton
was very proud of his mother—moments when
the years that were past rose up and rebuked
him for what they had lost, for the "might
have been" that yet never had been. Do not
the lives of men show many a ghostly harvest that has never been in-gathered and can
never be retrieved?

What little he could do to make up for the
past Lance faithfully set himself to do now;
but not much was possible. He was rarely
at the Old Hall, spending most of his time
with the Kynaston family, and absorbed in
the preparations for his mariage, after which
his home would be for a time in Italy

(Lady Jane having been delicate of late), and subsequently at a place called Allestrie, the Scotch seat of the Kynastons, a beautiful estate in the Lowlands. Besides preparations for these important changes, Lance appeared to have much and urgent business in London, a certain solicitor, by no means a man of the standing of the regular family lawyer, or even of "Old Medlicott," being also deeply concerned. There were long interviews and wordy wars, hours that seemed to steal from Launcelot's already worn and weary features the little light of gladness that was left to them. Then a hurried journey to Scarsdale, an interview with his father, a hurried return, and more interviews with the solicitor above named, who lived up a dreadful street looking on to the slow and sluggish river. This was a wearing enough life for any man. But the end came.

Some papers were signed; a deed of mortgage, old and yellowed by time, was handed to young Peyton; the stakes had been paid, the prize was won, but at what a cost!

Love, joy, the brightest things life can give, the purest pleasures a heart can know!

That a heavy sum of money, a sum that must eventually come out of his wife's fortune, was also sacrificed, galled Lance cruelly; not that he cared for the money for its own sake, but because it jarred against his sense of honour and right.

Yet, when even all this was done, the man whose cruel face had risen as one from the dead to confront Sir Marmaduke Peyton with the sin of his heedless youth; the hand that had clutched at name, fame, and position, threatening dishonour and disgrace to an ancient race, and sorrow and shame to the innocent wife and son, was not content.

"I might have asked more and got it," he said, snarling; and even the lawyer in questionable practice, who had been his agent in the matter, was repulsed by his vulpine greed, and glad to be able to retort—

"You might: you are not a man to stick at anything, and I, for one, am glad to be quit of the job. Why did you keep the deed back all these years? Why have you tortured the wretched man so cruelly?"

"It was like wine; it grew more valuable, would fetch a better price by keeping; and once, long since, when I held my head higher than now, when I had not——"

"Fallen so low," put in the other; "when you were not so well known on every race-course in the kingdom."

"Just so; he — Marmaduke Peyton — baulked me; he won the woman I wanted —the woman who would have kept me out of the mire, and made a different man of me. Worse still, I believe he has broken her heart. I caught a glimpse of her once when I was down that way."

"Threatening Sir Marmaduke with full exposure of that forged mortgage?"

"Exactly so; I caught a glimpse of her, and I tell you she is a broken-hearted woman. I owe him an extra twist of the screw for that. Still, if it hadn't been for her—for the sorrow and the misery that would have come upon her—I tell you I would not have foreclosed with this young fellow and saved the family name."

"You have feathered your nest pretty well, however; it will take this man several years to take up the bills he has signed in your favour."

"Yes, I was in desperate straits; and need and revenge form a strong cord when you twist them well together. That chip of the old block is going to marry a woman with fifty thousand pounds down, and the devil knows how much to come. I might have done better—I might have done better. I wish it was to come over again."

He pressed his hands hard together as though he were squeezing some yielding substance, then he stuck his heavy pocket-book into the breast-pocket of his overcoat, and shuffled—he had got past that stage when a man walks upright and looks his fellow-men in the face—out of the office into the busy bustling streets, as he passes out of the pages of our story.

Meanwhile, down at the old home, the

home that had tottered to its foundations, though its gentle mistress knew it not, Sir Marmaduke gave way to such a frenzy of unrestrained joy as none but a man who has found himself suddenly face to face with a risen sin, and lived for months the life of a hunted hare, knowing the danger past and the peril averted, can realise.

Lance could not bear the sight of the gleaming, eager eyes, the trembling hands outstretched. He gave up the yellow faded deed, that was snatched from his hold even in the giving, and, with one horror-struck look at the transformed man before him, hurried from the room. The door closed after him, the bolt of the lock shut into its rest, and in a few moments a little pile of grey ashes between the brass dogs of the wide-open fireplace of Sir Marmaduke's study was all that remained of a dead sin.

We must now retrace our steps a little to follow the fortunes of the curate of Scarsdale.

To his own mind they seemed but very

sorry fortunes indeed, as he wended his way
to the Rectory on one of the loveliest morn-
ings of the early year—a day that was a very
promise and forerunner of the earth's awakening.   Yet to Sleeksby Westerton no charm
lurked in the lilting of the birds, no pleasure
in the pale spears of the springing crocus or
the coy beauty of the modest snowdrop.

He was on his way to an interview that
he dreaded.   Weakness and vanity—two evil
guides enough for any man—had led him
among mires and quicksands ; yet he was not
so demoralised in mind as not to be able to
recognise the nature of the ground over which
he had travelled.

There had been of late something in the
Rector's eye, something in the Rector's manner,
that had caused Mr. Westerton deep-seated
uneasiness.   Other troubles, too, had come
upon him.   Estrangement and bitterness had
come about among—indeed, it may be said had
broken up—the "council of three."   No more
the curate dodged to get out of Sunday-school
or vestry in time to escape to the fastnesses of

the Meadows, and there lingeringly await the
arrival of sirens. No more he "wandered by
the mill," hushed to its Sunday rest while the
big wheel slowly dripped in solemn idleness
in its gloomy cave, accompanied by those
same bewildering charmers. A change had
come o'er the spirit of the Rev. Sleeksby's
dream ; in fact, a change had come o'er a good
many people's dreams, and it repented Mrs.
Mandeville that she had given so many confidences to the "friend of her soul."

As to Valerie, she grew desperate. In
moments of weakness she had—under vows
of silence most solemnly ratified—told various
female friends many things that Mr. Westerton had said, and, alas ! not a few things that
he had not said, and universal expectation
pointed to an anticipated engagement shortly
to be announced. As Valerie said bitterly to
herself, it was not even as if it was the first
time ; every one knew how ill—— But at this
point her maiden meditations would find vent
in tears. She appealed to Mrs. Mandeville.

"You are always telling me, Lottie, how

much a married woman can do ; cannot you do something to get him to explain this cruel estrangement ? "

Mrs. Mandeville, nothing loth, did her best.

" Mr. Westerton," she said, catching the helpless cleric at an awkward corner, where escape was well-nigh impossible, " what is the misunderstanding—the cloud—that has arisen between you and your best friends ? There are dreadful rumours abroad. Can it be true that you have fallen a prey to the designing—— No, no, Mr. Westerton, I *will* not believe it ! One word from you, and the hideous thought will be set at rest for ever. Speak—oh, speak that word ! "

He looked to this side and he looked to that. Never were more miserable looks cast appealingly at an unfeeling world over a clerical collar ; then, all at once, a glow suffused his face, a flash—actually a flash—illumined his lack-lustre eyes.

" Mrs. Mandeville," he said, " there is the Rector. I have to speak to him on parish

business—important business.   I wish you a
very good morning."

Never had the Scarsdale curate been so
delighted to see the Reverend the Rector of
Scarsdale !

Mr. Darling, for his part, noted that the
conference he had unwittingly interrupted
was "sadly borne," and that the curate flew
to his side like a fluttered chicken to the
mother's wing.   From these signs he drew
his own conclusions, but made no comment,
only intimating at the close of a "parish
talk" that Mr. Westerton should "step up"
to the Rectory the following afternoon, as
there was a little matter he wished to enter
upon.

That night the Rev. Sleeksby slept ill.
The expression "step up" seemed to have
taken hold upon him somehow, and he dreamt
—not that he dwelt in marble halls, far from
it—but that he was "stepping up" that uncomfortable machine the treadmill, which was,
by some strange freak of fortune, the mill-
wheel in the Meadows, housed in just such

a dingy archway. How the slimy revolving
stairs seemed to evade his eager feet! How
the damp and dripping walls failed him as he
tried to press his hands against their gruesome
grass-grown stones, and—was that the cackle
of fiendish laughter mocking his distress?

No; it was the sonorous quacking of his
landlady's ducks wading in the puddle beneath his window. The reverend gentleman
was awake once more; the rain-drops of the
night that was past glistened on the ivy-
leaves, the level sunrays of a new bright
day peered unpleasantly into his heavy eyes,
and he remembered that he was going to
"step up" to the Rectory that afternoon;
worse still, that he might have to face the
Rector's daughter, whose name he had made
so free with.

Meanwhile the news of utter defeat was
conveyed by Lottie to her Valerie, and Valerie
drooped like a creeper whose fastenings have
given way, so that it hangs limp and un-
sightly, a thing of nought before all men,
She cried with an exceeding bitter cry—

"He has behaved shamefully — he has behaved worse than any of the others!"

"There is treachery somewhere," said Mrs. Mandeville in her most awful manner.

Nor were things made any better by old Mandeville's coarse and unfeeling behaviour.

"What's come of the parson?" he said bluntly to his stony-eyed wife. "Why don't he come and get a dish of tea and a bite of victuals, same as he used to? I met him a couple of days ago looking mighty squirmy, and when I gave him a pleasant slap on the back, I thought I'd knocked his blessed soul out of his body. Lord, Lord! but he's a poor lot. Why, Ullathorne was worth fifty of him—ay, and fifty more to that. Bless my soul! wasn't it a game to see him make the ball fly on the cricket-meadow. Gad! I wish he was back amongst us again."

"Mr. Ullathorne had no soul," said Charlotte severely.

"No soul, hadn't he? Well, I'll bet my boots the fellows round here wished many a time he'd no body, or a less limber one,

anyway. If Ullathorne had got no soul,
then I like 'em made that way; and if this
flibberty-gibbet you women make so much of
has a soul, then that's the sort I don't like.
By the way, Lottie, don't you think it would
save a lot in shoe-leather to Miss Spider-legs
if she brought her bits o' duds and lived here
out and out?"

Mrs. Mandeville was apparently deaf. How,
indeed, else could a woman "with a soul"
answer such coarse invective than by a withering silence?

But her spouse wasn't withered a bit, not
he! He became jocose—to his wife's mind
his most repulsive frame of all.

"I say, Lottie, has Spider-legs been a bit
too loving and frightened his reverence?
Has he seen the small end of a noose, eh!
and gibbed? Young colts will sometimes,
you know. Poor Spider-legs! Poor old girl!
Baulked again, eh?"

Then he laughed—a soulless merriment,
that his wife, in her own mind, likened to the
crackling of thorns under a pot, and whipped

his bandana over his ribald old head, settling himself for a snooze.

We will now rejoin the Reverend Sleeksby "stepping up" to his interview with the Rector.

CHAPTER X.

"GANG AFT AGLEY."

As a beauty looks sweetest when she smiles
through her tears, so Scarsdale Rectory was
seen to its best advantage when the sunshine
glinted on tree and flower, hanging each and
all with diamonds, that sparkled and glittered
like gems. Even the chickens looked all the
better for a passing shower, and were as busy
as possible furbishing up their grey feather
coats and stroking down their pencilled
collars, while the pigeons each had a shadow
at its feet on the damp shining tiles, and
preened themselves, with melodious cooings,
in the welcome warmth.

Mr. Westerton did not preen himself, nor
yet did he coo. Indeed, his throat felt as if
it were lined with rusty nails, and his voice
was husky as he asked of the waiting-maid
if Mr. Darling was within.

Another moment and he was in the study, the rusty nails worse than ever, and a cold dew exuding from his manly brow.

How much did the Rector know? The case lay in that—in a nutshell, as it were —how much did the Rector know?

He was kindly and courteous—as at all times in his own house—with a touch of the courtliness of a day gone by; but Mr. Westerton missed the cordiality of the past, and the calm steady eyes had a look in their grey-blue depths that was not pleasant to meet—a look that made you feel like a sheet of plate-glass with no curtain drawn inside. There was no friendly inquiry after his (Mr. Westerton's) family, no interest shown in the course of reading necessary for his (Mr. Westerton's) preparation for the Bishop's examination for further Orders. It was all formal, a little stately, and beyond words embarrassing.

At length the crisis arrived.

"I will not make any pretence, Mr. Westerton," began the Rector, "of having asked you here this morning for the discussion of any ordinary parish matters. I may as well plunge *in medias res*, and say that I have been deeply troubled, cruelly hurt, during the past week."

"Dear me!" stammered the miserable Sleeksby; "I am truly sorry, truly grieved, Mr. Darling, to hear of this."

The rusty nails had by this time attained to such a pitch that he really thought his voice would fail him altogether. His hat, too, oppressed him. It made itself a very grasshopper of a hat, a burden hard to be borne, and his arms and legs were apparently ready to follow the bad example.

"Naturally," said the Rector, looking uncomfortably regal in his mighty high-backed chair, "naturally."

Now to have your loyalty taken for granted when you are inwardly conscious of having behaved like a perfect skunk is at no time pleasant. To Sleeksby Westerton it was simply torture.

He coloured so deeply that the tears rushed

into his eyes—a fact by no means unnoticed by the observant Rector.

"An outrage has been committed, Mr. Westerton—an outrage, in our midst."

This was so very unexpected that the curate nearly jumped out of his clothes, out of his skin, out of himself. His hat, which he had been holding uneasily in his hands (soft felt headgear did not exist among the clergy in those days, the regulation tall hat being the only thing permissible), slipped from his shaking fingers, and rolled ignominiously under the table, where at last it found a secure resting-place.

The Rector was too intent upon his subject to notice this freak of fortune, the curate too absorbed to pursue the fugitive. Mr. Westerton could only gasp by way of reply to the Rector's announcement. How he wished he had never wandered in the Meadows (accompanied by sirens); how he wished he had neither listened to confidences or given them ; most of all, oh! most of all, how he hated the folly that had led him to take the name of Alison Darling on his lips, and make it common sport "for daws to peck at!"

To make matters worse, just at that moment her graceful figure came into sight at the end of one of those soft green alleys that intersected the Rectory garden. She was walking slowly along, and to Mr. Westerton's eyes there seemed something of lassitude, of weariness in her gait.

"Have I brought about this sorrow by my folly? Is this my work?" he thought, and the thought stung. How beautiful, how desirable in every way appeared in his eyes that lovely old home, nestling amid its budding trees! How in a moment arose before him all the friendship and the hallowed companionship that might have been his—the jewels that he had bartered for base counterfeit!

"A letter—a base, unsigned letter—was sent to Sir Marmaduke. In that letter my daughter was cruelly impugned—accused of carrying on an intrigue, of making and keep-

ing assignations with Mr. Launcelot Peyton,
of doing all these things unknown to myself
and Sir Marmaduke, of being a plotter—an
ambitious plotter."

The Rector was warming with his theme.
His form seemed to dilate, his eyes to glow
like burning coals. Mr. Westerton could bear
no more.

"I swear," he cried, throwing himself, much
to the Rector's horror, on his knees on the
white goatskin rug before the fireplace, "that
I am innocent. I swear that I have had
no hand in this vile action. Bring any accusation against me but that! Oh, if only
my poor mother could see me at this moment,
whatever would she say?"

Then he fell a-weeping, and it must not
be taken as a slur upon the Reverend
Reginald Wentworth Darling's courage when
we say that an impulse of flight made itself
felt in his breast.

Mr. Sleeksby Westerton was not at any
time, perhaps, an inspiriting sight, but Mr.
Sleeksby Westerton damply weeping and on

his knees on the hearthrug was a sight to unnerve the strongest.

"My dear sir," said the Rector, with some agitation, "I never intended to hint at yours being the hand that played the traitor in such despicable fashion—never thought of such a thing! Nay, try to take a calm view of matters, and ask yourself, had even the very faintest suspicion of such a thing found a place in my mind, should I have asked you to visit me to-day, should I have allowed you to cross the threshold of my house? Rise, I pray you; rise and listen calmly to what I have to say, let me beg of you. Really, my dear sir!"

The Rector was genuinely distressed, and held out a helping hand to assist the unhappy man to rise. However, rising was one thing, and listening calmly another.

Mr. Westerton appeared to be absolutely incapable of gathering himself together. He had been foolish, weak, indiscreet, but he was a gentleman, and the idea that he might have had even ever so small a hand in the Rector's daughter being traduced, maligned, insulted, was unbearable.

"Mr. Westerton got up and began to "jump around," as the Americans have it, and the Rector was at a loss to decide whether his abasing of himself on the rug or his jumping around generally was the more distressful proceeding of the two.

"I really must beg of you," said Mr. Darling at last, turning his head from side to side to follow the gyrations of his guest —"I really must beg of you to desist, to be calm, to listen to reason. I cannot possibly say to you what I wish to say if you persist in behaving in this absurd manner. Your own common-sense——"

But here the Rector paused.

He felt the absurdity of his own appeal. Mr. Westerton had no common-sense; of what use, then, to appeal to that which did not exist?

Suddenly the Rector bethought himself of firmer ground whereon to plant appeal.

"Mr. Westerton," he said, "my wife is,

as you know, a sufferer. I fear she will hear this" (he was going to say "uproar," but replaced it by the more delicate word " disturbance ") — " this disturbance, and it will——"

" Forgive me," said poor Sleeksby, wiping his heated brow, and throwing himself all limp and dejected into a chair. " I am thoughtless as usual. The fact is, I have gone through a good deal—passed through many most trying experiences—of late, and I am unnerved, Mr. Darling—pitiably unnerved. I start at my own shadow, or anybody else's, for the matter of that; if a knock comes at the door, it goes down my spine—it does indeed; and now whatever remnant of nerves are left to me will be shattered, broken up, destroyed for ever. If my poor mother could know the state I'm in, whatever would she say ? "

" There is no need—there is really no need at all to trouble—er—Mrs. Stanley Westerton or my good friend your worthy father about the—er—mischances that have come about in consequence, as I am convinced, of a—well, let us say a want of due reticence on your part—a folly—a——"

Dear, dear, if only the man had been the son of anybody else but the friend who watched over him so tenderly in time of sore illness in the dear old Oxford days, how much, *much* easier the Rector's task would have been!

The word that suited the occasion was *lâcheté*, but how to hurl it at the head of Stanley Westerton's son?

Taking the law of heredity into his own hands, how often had Mr. Darling said to himself during the period of Sleeksby's diaconate, "Stanley must have married a fool!" for the friends had drifted—Mr. Westerton to a foreign chaplaincy, the other to quiet, lovely Scarsdale-in-the-Dales.

"I have, I have indeed," said Mr. Westerton, in reply to the Rector's only half-completed sentence. "I know what you allude to perfectly, perfectly. I met Miss Alison; I met her under peculiar—under most trying circumstances. In my vanity and folly I mentioned these—these circumstances."

The Rector's hand was uplifted to enjoin silence. The Rector coloured high.

"Mr. Westerton, you are about to be indiscreet again. Spare me the mention of names, I beg. I do not wish to have my thoughts directed into any special quarter. I prefer not. There are things in life that it is well never to know, that we may pray to be kept from knowing. When we love deeply there are injuries it is almost impossible to forgive, and an unpardoned injury is a scar on the heart of a Christian. Suffice, then, for me to say that it is evident you have been imprudent—nay (I am sorry to have to say this to your father's son), disloyal, and indirectly, and, I am well convinced, with no intention, brought much suffering upon an innocent girl. I have thought it best to send for you, and to tell you all the truth, to give you the fullest explanation of what you saw and what you must have spoken of."

We have given such a description of Mr. Westerton's miserable condition that it seems hardly possible to describe him as in any lower depth. Perhaps there is a certain comfort in having attained to a dead level of misery, a content similar to that of lying down all along upon the ground—you can fall no lower.

"I would much rather not hear anything more; indeed, indeed I stand in no need of any explanation at all. I have made a miserable ass of myself; I have made a miserable cur of myself. I did meet Miss Alison and the gentleman in question. I did mention the matter. Mr. Darling, what am I to say? What *can* I say to you?"

"Say nothing; rather listen, and then (I speak as to the son of my dear old friend your father) let the past be a lesson for the future. Try to realise that in our profession above all others, silence is golden. It is hard, I know, very often for a parish priest to keep himself clear of parish gossip; and perhaps at times I have erred in trying to stand too

much aloof from my people in this respect,
and thus lost the chance of giving a friendly
hint to those to whom a friendly hint might
have been helpful."

"Meaning me, Mr. Darling," put in the
wretched Westerton, "meaning me. Oh,
dear, if my poor mother could only know
what a fool I have made of myself since
I came to this place, whatever would she
say?"

"Let us hope she may never know," said
the Rector, with some difficulty looking as
stern as he felt the occasion demanded (it is
hard to deal severely with mere pulp), "let
us hope so. Believe me, Mr. Westerton, that
in the multitude of female counsellors many
a man placed as you are makes shipwreck of
himself and his sacred calling. Remember
that it is only very exceptional women who
are to be trusted with a man's entire confidence, and that such women are rare. I do
not want to conceal from you that there has
been sorrow and trouble between my dear
daughter and her old playfellow. Young

men and women do not always know their
own hearts, and an unguarded moment may
overtake any one of us."

"Yes, oh, yes; it may indeed," said poor
Sleeksby, as though the barbed saying came
home to him in a peculiarly pointed manner;
"it may indeed."

"Such a moment came to them, one of
them being no longer free—in fact, bound in
all honour, as, indeed, all the world by this
time knows. Of course, when you——"

"Made a fool and a cur of myself."

The Rector smiled a little smile of assent,
then continued—

"When you were indiscreet enough to
speak of a thing that had come to your
knowledge entirely by accident, you had
(as I am well convinced) no slightest intention of bringing outrage and misconstruction
upon——"

"If I knew," began Mr. Westerton, grasp-
ing his umbrella in both hands and raising it
weapon-wise to annihilate an imaginary foe,—
"if I only knew . . . ."

"Yes, yes," said the Rector, gently impatient, "we all feel like that at times, but it does no good, you know; and besides, you don't know, neither do I; we do not want to know."

Mr. Westerton looked mutinous, but, awed to silence, lowered his weapon.

"What I want to come to is this," continued Mr. Darling, feeling, it must be confessed, some little difficulty in approaching the critical point. "I am convinced that, with fresh surroundings, disencumbered of— er—entanglements, shall we say, without which your course and action in life would be freer, more spontaneous, less hampered, as it were——"

Oh, those sirens, those sirens! what trouble they had brought upon the Reverend Sleeksby Westerton! Rambles by river and by mead, delightful flutterings of little confidential notes and messages, "diary of my soul," and all the rest of it, how dearly were you bought, how dearly have you cost! And now, how shall the distressed one tell his chief that he has become tied, bound, compassed about in life and limb by the closest "entanglement" of all, that he almost has a fit if he sees the fair Valerie in the distance, and that the sight of Mrs. Mandeville causes him to fall into a cold sweat?

"Mr. Darling," he said, and the rusty nails grew worse and worse till they formed a sort of *chevaux de frise* through which the breath came whistling, "I shall not be likely to fall again into the folly that I have been guilty of at Scarsdale. I am going to be married. I am engaged to Mrs. Barnstaple-Ambler, and she wishes the—the ceremony to be— to be——"

"Bless my soul!" cried the Rector, quite losing all trace of his usual self-command, and betraying an almost wild amazement. "Why, she's forty if she's a day; and you, Mr. Westerton, are still almost a boy. Dear, dear! I beg your pardon; I fear I am being very rude. I was so completely taken aback, you really must pardon me."

"What you say is quite true," put in

Sleeksby; "and I see no offence in it. She is more than forty; but permit me to suggest, sir, that she is a fine figure of a woman, and I feel convinced she will take every care of me, I do indeed."

The Rector put his hand to his forehead for a moment as if to help himself to realise facts, and then a bright thought struck him.

Tea—yes, tea was the thing. Under the circumstances Mr. Westerton must stand in need of consolation of some sort, and tea—yes, certainly tea was the thing.

He put his hand on the curate's shoulder.

"Come," he said, "let Alison give you some tea."

Sleeksby appeared to him all at once in the light of a child who stood in need of kindness and protection. He could not recover his calm and dignity at all.

"Bless my soul!" he muttered. "Bless my soul! Well, well! Dear me, dear me!"

But a man had arisen in Mr. Westerton different altogether from the man he seemed to be.

Tea was a thing—for the present, at all events—not to be thought of. Mr. Westerton was about to assert himself. A rabbit—gentlest, most simple of beasts—will stamp with its hind-legs when it is fully roused. Mr. Westerton was, figuratively speaking, going to stamp with his hind-legs.

He drew himself away from the kindly hand; he backed as far as the wall. In trying moments it is well to have some extraneous support. He made a valiant effort and swallowed some of the rusty nails, an exertion that made the tears come into his eyes.

"Mr. Darling," he said, "you were going to say something else when this—this change in my prospects cropped up, and put everything else out of your head. I know what you were going to say. I think you are quite right. You were going to say it would be better for me to leave Scarsdale. If you will only be so good as sanction my application to the Bishop for permission to go now, at once, as soon as I can get another curacy, I shall be grateful—

deeply, deeply grateful to you. Sophonia—
Sophonia is Mrs. Barnstaple-Ambler—will be
deeply grateful also. She is of opinion that
I cannot make the move too soon—for various
reasons. Sophonia said that she should like
you to—to, in fact, tie the nuptial knot.
I, too——"

"Mr. Westerton," said the Rector, who
had during this somewhat lengthy harangue
rumpled his wavy locks into a most unusual
degree of disorder, "I will do anything I can
to help you. I doubt not the future will
bring——"

But here he thought of Sophonia, and
choked.

When Mr. Westerton's mother knew that
her angel Sleeksby was going to marry a
widow over forty (even though her figure was
undeniable), whatever would she say?

This thought ran in a mild sort of riot in
the Rector's mind, amid the chink of tea-
spoons and the ripple of quiet talk that
followed the entrance of the two black-coated
figures into Mrs. Darling's room.

Mr. Westerton felt guilty and miserable, but he was glad of the tea, as it washed away some of the rusty nails. His hand trembled as he took his tea from Alison, so that the cup danced quite a fandango in the saucer. He could not help but see how the girl's face was changed; her cheek was pale, and there were purple rings round her beautiful eyes— the eyes that looked at him so kindly, so forgivingly—and that were yet, oh! so sad when you looked close at them.

Even obtuse Mr. Westerton quickly realised the fact that Mrs. Darling was in perfect ignorance of the trouble that had come upon and hit the other two. She was better than usual, serene as a pool of still water with the sun shining on it, and as bright; spoke of Lance Peyton's engagement to the Lady Jane, and how a friend in London had written in the highest terms of the bride-elect.

Not a quiver in Alison's face told that her mother's words stung; and if any one changed colour, it was Mr. Westerton himself. The self-discipline that is practised daily seldom

fails when any sudden strain is put upon it;
"Ready, aye ready," is its motto.

Nothing could exceed the matter-of-fact
manner in which the Rector spoke of the
whole affair; and he patted his wife's hand
and said she was "as fond of a bit of a stir
as the youngest," when that sweet lady ex-
pressed a hope that they would see some of
the wedding finery down at Scarsdale, and
that the village would be *en fête*.

The comedy was so perfectly acted that
who could imagine all the tragedy that lay
beneath it?

Not a word said the Rector of the news
just imparted to him. Mrs. Barnstaple-
Ambler might never have existed for any
allusion that was made to her, and for once
Mr. Westerton was endowed also with tact,
and spake no word of his Sophonia. After
the curate had gone, and when Mrs. Darling
was taking the rest that always followed the
evening meal, Alison went to her father's
study. She stood by the table, her hand
resting lightly upon it. The light had died

out of her face, the elasticity was gone from her tread; she was not before the footlights now, but face to face with the one who could read all her heart and gauge all her sorrow.

"Papa," she said, "I suppose it was Mr. Westerton?"

"Yes, my dear; he has been greatly to blame; but he is very sorry—he is, in fact, overwhelmed—he is indeed; and, Alison, he is going to marry Mrs. Barnstaple-Ambler."

"Then he will get into no more mischief," said Alison, her lip quivering to a smile.

"Poor little man!" said the Rector; and Scarsdale echoed the sentiment when a day or two later the great news was made public property.

As to Valerie, she observed a dignified silence, while a tinge of extra bitterness was added to Mrs. Mandeville's seething indignation by the indecent behaviour of her husband, who slapped his thigh and shook his fat sides, crying that the widow "banged creation," and Spider-legs was nowhere; indeed, chuckled himself almost into a fit, and until

the tears ran down his face, bursting out
anew, and yet again, just when his wife
thought and hoped the revolting scene was
over.

He vowed he'd go and "see the pair turned
off." He met Mr. Westerton, and slapped
him on the back so that the curate's heart
seemed to leap into his mouth like a plum.
He congratulated him in such a loud tone
that the people coming in by Jollick's stopped
to listen; the driver grinned, and the boy
with the horn had to bury his head in the
boot among the parcels to keep from laughing
outright. He vowed the widow was a fine
woman, and poked the blushing Sleeksby in
the ribs.

When he got home, he told his wife what he
had done, and the "diary of the soul" had
seventeen pages added to it that night. But,
alas! there was no kindred spirit, no spiritual
sympathiser near to read the pitiful narrative
of a heart's trials.

A guarded note, in which she wished her
"once kind friend" adieu, bidding him not

garner up his hopes too closely on any earthly
prospect of delight, was all Mrs. Mandeville
dare venture upon to the traitor Sleeksby ;
while poor Valerie, hampered by her virgin
state and the *convenances* that beset a female
so circumstanced, could only beg for a little
message to be included on her behalf—a little
timid, trembling message, hinting that for her
the world would henceforth be a blank.

Soon—marvellously soon it seemed to some
people—Scarsdale knew Sleeksby Westerton
no more. There were not wanting those who
said that Mrs. Barnstaple-Ambler "whipped
him up and carried him off;" but no one
really knew how things were, for the nuptial
knot was not tied at the church of the
taper spire and the sweet far-sounding bells,
after all.

"To Let" appeared on a drunken-looking
board, that apparently could not be induced
to stand upright by any means known to
mortal man, in the pretty garden sheltered
by the ivy-covered wall, lolling negligently
towards the street, as who should say—

" If you like to come and look at this house, you can; but I don't think much of it myself, and don't advise you to do so," which was perhaps the reason why Mrs. Barnstaple-Ambler's late abode remained some length of time untenanted.

Some folks were sorry to lose Mr. Westerton. They said he was a " kindly sort of creature," and would have done well enough if the ladies had let him alone. But the notes of admiration and regret were feeble and halting; and, on the other side, Maister Straw and Pilkington gave tongue loudly, being for once agreed.

"Doan't tell me!" said Master Straw. " He wur a mon o' very small account, wur Maister Westerton; an' it's my belief as yo' couldna make a gentleman o' him—no, not if you skinned him. He wur full oop wi' petty talk an' women's nonsense an' whisperin's, an' such like. Now Maister Ullathorne wur the mon for me; he wur a mon, an' a man o' God too; and as for them lions i' the path, he smote 'em hip and thigh, as the Scripter hath it. But for this one," here Jonathan

flicked his fingers to show the flimsy nature
of Mr. Ullathorne's successor, "he wur too
much given to dulcimers, an' tea-meetin's,
an' twinkling symbols, an' all such like;" to
which opinion Pilkington gave a solemn nod
of assent.

And thus the Reverend Sleeksby Westerton
passes from Scarsdale for ever, let us hope to
spend many happy years by the side of his
Sophonia.

The arrival of his successor (oh! the charm
of newness!) was a day of much interest in
Scarsdale, for to "sit upon" and "judge"
clergy is one of the keenest pleasures known
to the rustic mind.

"What do you think of 'un now?" is a
question that has a never-dying charm, and
one may be sure the oak-tree parliament was
in full vogue and swing. The ladies of the
congregation were not so much on the *qui
vive*, for the new curate was married—very
much married, as it turned out, since he and
his wife stumped the country linked arm-in-
arm in search of natural history specimens, in

which science the gentleman was an enthusiast,
and never seemed to know what it was to be
tired. A couple of wiry little people, having
worked long and hard in a densely populated
town, they revelled in the greenery of fields
and lanes, and were always looking over gates
at views in the distance, or getting into soft
and sludgy places after rare ferns or peculiar
moths.

A fair reader; a preacher that grew upon
you; a man gifted with tender, helpful sympathy by the sick-bed or face to face with the
stricken in heart—what more could a little
country town expect? From the day when
that monster Jollick's vomited them forth
outside the Golden Crown, the little couple
seemed to glide into their places in the village
community as if their niches had been ready
and they had just stepped into them. The
husband was soon brimful of enthusiasm about
the church—hence the Rector "cottoned" to
him at once, and he speedily worshipped the
Rector. The wife was full of pretty devices
to interest Mrs. Darling, in drying flowers in

such a manner as to preserve their colour,
and various kindred matters—hence Alison
took to her amazingly. So there came an
added brightness to the dear old Rectory from
the newcomers; and though "papa" never
said so, his daughter was convinced he felt
the departure of Mr. Westerton to be a
relief.

These changes were not wrought in a day.
The corn grew golden in the lovely Yorkshire
dales, the sheaves were garnered in, the link
grew purple on the upland slopes, and then
the tracery of bare brown boughs showed like
etchings against the sky; the woods were
silent under their burden of snow, and the
Christmas roses nodded in the keen frosty
air before things settled down into the old
jog-trot, and Maister Straw was ready to
declare that there was no "new curate" at
Scarsdale, for the one they had might have
been there "twenty years and more," so
"homely" was he with them all.

The people at the Old Hall had been much
away since the marriage of Lance in the

autumn, Sir Marmaduke and Lady Peyton travelling abroad; but now they were all home for the coming Christmas-tide, and the Rector fancied he noticed a deeper peace, even a flickering brightness, in the face of the woman who had drunk so deeply of the cup of sorrow.

He said to himself that this might be only his fancy; but at last he knew that it was reality, for Lady Peyton spoke to him of herself—a rare thing indeed, and one fated to be impressed upon his mind in characters indelible and fadeless. They were standing in the churchyard, and the evening was what is called in country places a "rosy" one—that is, above the snow-clad world shone a sky of faint clear ruby, the sign and harbinger of coming frost. Against this beauteous glow the branches of the tall trees, glistening with hoar-frost, showed like jewelled sceptres, and, to make all things perfect, within the church the choir were practising the Christmas hymns, and the mingled voices, softened by the closed doors, came stealing out across the graves as though telling of a life and hope beyond the tomb.

A tremulous light of joy was on Lady Peyton's face, a dewy brightness as of tears ready to start in her deep-set eyes.

"I have had such a beautiful Christmas gift," she said, laying her hand on the Rector's arm, and looking up into his face.

There was something so holy in her chastened joy that the Rector felt as though he stood within a sanctuary. He uncovered, and so stood bareheaded as she said—

"The 97th is ordered to Gibraltar. I suppose it does not *really* make any very great difference, but it seems ever so much nearer, almost like having my Cyril given back to me."

END OF VOL. I.

Printed by BALLANTYNE, HANSON & CO
Edinburgh and London

www.ingramcontent.com/pod-product-compliance
Lightning Source LLC
Chambersburg PA
CBHW060539030726
47498CB00004B/1250